DISNEY

MALEFICENT

MISTRESS OF EVIL

HEART of the MOORS

HEART of the MOORS

HOLLY BLACK

LOS ANGELES • NEW YORK

Printed in the United States of America
First Hardcover Edition, October 2019
1 3 5 7 9 10 8 6 4 2
FAC-020093-19249

Library of Congress Control Number: 2019944069
ISBN 978-1-368-04561-2

disneybooks.com

FOR EVERYONE WHO HAS DELIGHTED
IN THEIR OWN PAIR OF HORNS
—HB

PROLOGUE

"Once upon a time, there was a wicked faerie called Maleficent, named for both her malice and her magnificence. Her lips were the red of freshly spilled blood, her cheekbones as sharp as the pain of lost love. And her heart was as cold as the deepest part of the ocean."

The storyteller stood on a cobbled street near the castle, watching with satisfaction as a crowd formed. Children peered up at him openmouthed, henwives stopped in the middle of their shopping, and tradespeople drew close.

Among them was a woman shrouded in a hooded cloak.

She stood slightly apart, and even though he couldn't see her face, something about her drew his eye.

The storyteller had crossed into the kingdom of Perceforest just two days before, and his tale had gotten a good reception in the previous town. Not only had he made a pocketful of copper, but he had been stood a supper at the second-best inn and offered a place by the fire that night. Surely, so near the castle, where there was bound to be more coin, his tale would earn him even greater rewards.

"There was a princess, Aurora, named for the dawn. Her hair was as golden as the crown that would one day rest upon her head. Her eyes were as wide and soft as those of a doe. From the time of her birth, no one could look upon her and not love her. But the wicked faerie hated goodness and put her under a curse."

All around him, the listeners sucked in their breath. The storyteller was pleased until he realized that they looked alarmed in a way that didn't seem entirely pleasurable. Something was wrong, but he wasn't sure what it could be. He had heard a variation of this story all the way out in Weaverton and had taken it upon himself to embroider it a bit. He was sure it was a solid tale, one crafted to flatter the prejudices of the old and inflame the passions of the young.

"Upon her sixteenth birthday, she was to prick her finger on a spindle and die!"

Several listeners cried out in dismay. One of the children clutched another's hand.

Again, that reaction wasn't quite right. It shouldn't affect them so greatly.

It was clearly time to temper the villainy of his tale with a sprinkle of heroism. "But you see, there was a good faerie and—"

A snort came from the hooded figure. The storyteller paused, ruining the momentum of his tale. He was about to pick up the threads and start again when the cloaked woman spoke.

"Is that what happened?" Her voice was melodious, with traces of an accent he couldn't place. "Truly? Are you *sure*, storyteller?"

He'd dealt with hecklers before. He gave her his brightest smile, looking around, inviting the crowd to smile with him. "Every word is as true as your standing before me."

"What would you wager on that?" came the voice. He realized his audience was riveted by this exchange, far more than they had been by his story. "Would you give me your voice? Your firstborn? Your life?"

He laughed nervously.

The woman threw off her cloak, and he took an involuntary step away from her. And then another.

The crowd shrank back in anticipatory horror.

"You—you—" He couldn't get the words out.

Black horns as sinister as her smile curved back from her head. Her lips were the red of freshly spilled blood. Her cheekbones were as sharp as the pain of lost love. And he was afraid that her heart was indeed as cold as the deepest part of the ocean.

Suddenly, it struck the storyteller that tales all came from somewhere. And that Perceforest was rumored to have a very young queen, one whose name he hadn't thought to ask but was beginning to guess. Which meant that standing in front of him was . . .

"You must have guessed my name, storyteller. Won't you tell me yours?" Maleficent asked.

But it seemed he couldn't make his mouth work.

She waited a moment, and then her lips curled up into a smile that promised nothing good. "No? No matter. Let this be your fate: *You shall be a cat,* yowling your stories under windows but never having the satisfaction of getting better than a thrown boot or water dumped on your head for your trouble. Let you remain so until my wicked heart relents."

Maleficent's hands sent a whirl of glittering golden

light at him, and everyone around the storyteller began to grow. Even the screaming children became enormous, their worn leather shoes the size of his head. He fell to his hands and knees. A curious warmth covered him, as though someone had thrown a fur blanket across his back. He opened his mouth to cry out, but the sound that came from him was a terrible, inhuman yowling.

"I believe you already know the end of the story," Maleficent said to the crowd. Then she leaped into the sky, her large and powerful wings carrying her away from town in a rush of wind—leaving the storyteller, who had made his living from words, no longer able to speak a one.

1

When Aurora had been a child in the forest
and her only crown had been woven of
honeysuckle, she'd thought that the queen of the distant
castle must be happy all the time, because everyone had to
listen to her and do exactly what she said. Since Aurora
had come to the throne, she'd discovered just how wrong
she'd been.

For one thing, now everyone seemed to want to tell
her what to do.

Her late father's advisor, a grim-faced elderly man
called Lord Ortolan, liked to drone on and on about her

royal obligations, which usually involved enacting his strategies for enriching the treasury.

And there were the courtiers—young men and women from noble families throughout the kingdom sent to the palace to be her companions. They took for granted luxuries and delights she'd never known. They taught her formal dances she'd never tried before, and brought in minstrels to sing songs of heroic deeds, and jugglers and acrobats to make her laugh with their antics. They gossiped about one another and speculated about Prince Phillip's extended visit to her kingdom and whether his pretext of studying Ulsteadian folklore in the libraries of Perceforest was his real reason for remaining. It was all very pleasant, but they still wanted her to do things the way they had always been done. And Aurora wanted change.

She might have expected her godmother, Maleficent, to be sympathetic, but she wasn't. Instead, Maleficent made endless unhelpful and pointed suggestions about how Aurora would be happier ruling her kingdom from the Moors. And while Aurora lived at the palace, Maleficent stayed away. For the first time in her life, Aurora didn't have the comfort of Maleficent's shadow.

It didn't help that Aurora *would* be happier in the Moors. The castle was massive and drafty and damp. Wind often whistled down interior corridors. The fireplaces were fond of backing up, giving the elaborately decorated rooms a slight but constant stink of smoke. Worst of all, though, was the iron. Iron latches, iron bars on windows, and iron bands on doors. They were a reminder of the horrible things her father, King Stefan, had done and the even more horrible things he'd wanted to do. Aurora had ordered it all stripped and replaced, but that was such a large undertaking that not even a quarter of the rooms were finished.

She didn't blame Maleficent for not wanting to visit her there, with all those memories.

But the palace was where Aurora needed to be. Not just because she wanted to know what it was like to be human, but because she had one goal as queen of Perceforest and the Moors—to lead the faeries and humans of both kingdoms into thinking of themselves as belonging to one united land. Her first step was a treaty. The only problem was that no one could agree on anything.

The faeries wanted the humans to stay out of the Moors, but wanted to be able to wander through Perceforest whenever they liked. And the humans wanted to be able to pick up whatever they found lying around in the Moors, even though some of those things were actually mushroom faeries, or crystals that were part of the landscape, or bits of other creatures' homes.

She had spent the morning trying to make headway, to no avail.

"I hope no one here has offended you," said Count Alain, drawing Aurora out of her wandering thoughts. The youngest of her important landholders, he was also the most dashing. He had thick midnight hair with a single stripe of white in it, like a very handsome skunk.

"Excuse me?" Aurora asked, puzzled.

He pointed toward the window. "You've put a terror in all of us that you might glare at us the way you've been glaring at that window."

"Oh, no," she said, embarrassed. "I was only lost in my own contemplations."

On the other side of the great hall, a harpist was entertaining a group of ladies. The royal household had come from their midday dinner and were beginning to consider the games and activities of the evening.

Count Alain stroked his chin, where a thin beard grew. His green eyes sparked with mirth, but sometimes she wondered if he was laughing at her. "I fear we have neglected to amuse you, my queen. Let's have a hunt in those woods you were staring at."

"That's very kind," Aurora replied, "but I have never liked hunting. I feel too sorry for the creatures."

"Your sympathy does you credit," Count Alain said, and before she could respond, he broke into a wide grin. "Yet this you will enjoy! It will be all in fun. A mere excuse for a romp. Surely you'd like to get out of this stuffy castle for a pleasant afternoon."

She *did* want to get out of the castle.

"Yes," said a voice. It was Prince Phillip, just entering the room, mud on his boots. "I can testify you ought to, Your Majesty. Your kingdom is marvelously beautiful right now, with summer turning to autumn."

With his caramel curls and a careless smile he bestowed on everyone, he turned the heads of most of the women and half the men in the room.

But not hers. Since she had become queen, he was the one she confided in, the one she laughed with when she felt overwhelmed by the task of ruling the kingdom. Just the night before, they'd spent a comfortable evening playing the Game of the Goose in front of the fire, both of them cheating unmercifully.

Friendship with Prince Phillip was safe. He'd already kissed her, after all, even if she didn't remember it. And he hadn't even done it because he *wanted* to, but in the hopes it might end the curse.

It hadn't, because he didn't love her. It hadn't been

True Love's Kiss—which, she told herself, was a relief. After all, love had been the cause of all of Maleficent's pain. Friendship was better in every way.

"Tell me this," she said to Phillip. "In your land, is hunting ever done *all in fun*?"

"In Ulstead," he said after giving the matter some thought, "while many find hunting enjoyable, we always do it in deadly earnest."

Aurora turned back to Count Alain. His smile had stiffened. She felt a little guilty.

"I would love to ride in the forest," Aurora told him. "But it must not be a hunt. And we must not cross into the Moors."

"Of course, my queen," replied Count Alain, the spark back in his eyes. "It is well known you take an unaccountably generous view of the faeries."

Her instinct was to snap at Count Alain that it was the *humans* who had waged war against the Fair Folk for generations and not the other way around, but she bit back the words. He had grown up being warned about the Moors. Like most of the nobility, he had no experience with the beauty of the place—or the joyful wildness of the beings who lived there.

He'd grown up with lies. She had to convince him that what he'd heard was wrong and believe that he could learn a new way of seeing the faeries. A new way of seeing the world.

If she could get him on her side, he would be a powerfully ally in negotiating the treaty and in changing the minds of her people, especially the younger courtiers, who admired him.

Perhaps the ride was a *very* good idea.

"We must not cross into the Moors, but we can ride close enough to view them," Aurora amended. "In fact, the whole court ought to come. We can go tomorrow afternoon and picnic up high enough that we can see inside. The Moors are nothing like the wall of briars that used to surround them. They're beautiful."

Count Alain sighed and gave a smile that was only a little forced. "As you wish, my queen."

2

W ould you like to know what it's like to lose your wings?

First you have to imagine tasting clouds on your tongue and diving through the sky as you might dive into a pool of water on a hot summer day.

You have to imagine the sun on your face when you're above the clouds.

You have to imagine never having to be afraid of heights.

And the wings themselves, folded on your back, soft

and downy. You have slept every night of your life covered in their warmth.

Then they're gone. Cut away. A part of you missing, a part that's still alive and beating against a cage you can't see.

You feel a raw pain. You are a wound that never closes.

You become plodding and slow. The kingdom you've lost is above you, cerulean and out of reach.

You curse the sky.

Curse the air.

Curse the girl.

And then you become the curse.

3

Aurora hated to sleep. Every night she made excuses to stay up later and later. There were always lists to make, letters to write, endless revisions of the treaty to puzzle over. She wandered around her enormous chamber, stoking the fire and letting her candles burn down so low each wick guttered out in a pool of wax.

But there always came a point when she had to put on her smock and cap and blow out her candle. Then she huddled under her blankets and looked out her window at the stars, trying to convince herself that it was safe to close her eyes, that she would wake up in the morning.

She wasn't going to sleep for a hundred years.

The enchantment was gone.

The curse was broken.

But most nights Aurora only fell asleep to the pink of dawn blushing on the horizon. Most days she woke up exhausted. Some days she could barely get up.

Yet when the next night came, the fear struck her anew. Falling asleep felt like falling down a deep well, one that she might never claw her way out of.

After tossing and turning for what felt like ages that evening, she got out of bed. Throwing on a heavy gold brocade robe over her smock, she padded through the silent, sleeping household to a fountain on the edge of the royal gardens.

Phillip looked up from where he was sitting, whittling a little flute in the moonlight. "Your Majesty," he said. "I was hoping you'd come."

The first time she'd stumbled on him during one of her evening walks, he'd told her that in Ulstead, court parties lasted all night, and he'd grown used to keeping late hours. That time, they'd skipped rocks on an ornamental pond.

"It's the treaty keeping me up," she told him with a

sigh, although it wasn't the whole truth. "I'm afraid that the humans and the faeries will never agree to anything. And if I force them, then what's the use?"

"In Ulstead, the stories of faeries are even worse than those told here, and there are no Fair Folk to contradict them. The kinder tales are no longer told. The only place to even find them is in the Ulsteadian section of your royal library. The people of Perceforest are fortunate, even if they haven't quite realized it yet."

Aurora was surprised. "Did *you* believe those stories?"

Phillip glanced toward the woods. "Until I came here, I had stopped believing in faeries at all." Then he turned back to her with a smile. "Everything new is hard. But you have a way of making people listen. You'll convince them."

She shook her head at his kind words, but they made her feel better. "I hope so. And since I am so convincing, maybe I can convince you not to cheat at a game of moonlight loggets."

"It's impossible to cheat at throwing sticks!" he exclaimed, although he was already looking around for the best fallen branch to grab.

"We shall see," she promised, snatching the stick he'd been eyeing.

That led to a mad laughing scramble. Phillip tried to

yank the stick out of Aurora's hands. Aurora tugged back. But then the stick broke and she landed on the ground.

Phillip looked horrified. "Your pardon," he said, reaching down a hand. "My behavior was most ungentlemanly."

Standing, Aurora dusted off her brocade robe. She felt foolish.

She wanted to tease him. She wanted him to laugh again. She wanted to remind him that they were friends, and friends were allowed to be silly with each other, even if one of them was a queen and the other a prince.

But looking into his eyes, she couldn't find the right words.

"Let me walk you back to the palace," he said, offering her his arm and a slightly uncertain smile. "And as a sign of my contrition, I will attempt not to steer you into a ditch."

"Perhaps I should be the one to steer," Aurora said lightly.

"Without a doubt," Phillip returned.

Too early, the curtains were parted and sunlight streamed in. Aurora groaned and tried to bury her head beneath her pillows.

Her chambermaid, Marjory, set down a tray on the

end of the bed. Tea, bread and butter, and quince jam.

"Though it's very improper, your advisor insisted I tell you he would like an audience as soon as you were up," the girl said, turning to shake out a dress of celery green.

"What do you suppose he wants?" Aurora asked, pushing herself into a sitting position. She took the warm cup and brought it to her lips. Despite having lived in the castle for months, she refused to ignore her servants as the other nobles told her was proper. Her father had been a servant in the castle before he was king, and for all his faults, Aurora felt his rise ought to have proven that no one should be overlooked. "Sit with me. Eat some bread and jam."

Marjory sat readily, but she didn't appear to be her usual cheerful self. She was a redhead with very pale freckled skin that grew flushed and blotchy when something upset her, as it apparently had. "Some of the townsfolk have been waiting to see you. Lord Ortolan tried to send them away, but they refuse to go."

"So you think that's what he wants to discuss?" Aurora buttered two slices of the bread and pushed one toward Marjory.

The girl took a big bite. "Well, Nanny Stoat says that Lord Ortolan doesn't want you to talk to *any* of your people but those who are in his pocket. Forgive me for repeating this, but she says he doesn't want you to have any ideas that he didn't give you."

"Nanny Stoat?" Aurora asked.

"Everyone in the village listens to her," Marjory said. "If there's a problem, people say, 'Take it to Nanny Stoat,' because she'll figure out how to make it right."

"So you think Lord Ortolan *doesn't* plan to tell me about the townsfolk?" Aurora asked. "And that he will continue to try to send them away?"

Marjory nodded, although she looked guilty as she did so.

Aurora downed the rest of her tea and got out of bed. She went to her dressing table and started brushing out her hair roughly. "I'd better get down there immediately if I want to speak with them. Tell me anything else you've heard—rumors, anything!"

"Wait!" said Marjory, jumping off the bed and forcibly taking the brush from Aurora's hand. "I'll braid up your hair as swiftly as I can if you stop doing *that* to it."

"Do you know what they want?" Aurora asked, sitting and scowling at herself in the mirror.

The girl began to detangle her hair, separating it down the middle with a clean part. "I heard there was a missing boy. A servant here in the castle. He was one of the grooms, so I didn't know him particularly."

Aurora turned in her chair. "Missing? What do you mean?"

"He walked home to see his mother," Marjory said, valiantly holding on to the sections of hair she'd been braiding, "but he never got there, and no one has seen him since."

A few minutes later, Aurora ran down the stairs in silken slippers and the green gown.

Lord Ortolan tried to interrupt her as she marched toward the palace doors. "Your Majesty, I am so glad you're up. If I could command your attention for a moment, there's a matter of some magical flora along the border—"

"I would like to speak with the family of the missing boy," she said.

His surprise was evident. "But how did you know?"

"That's not important," she said as pleasantly as she could, "since it saves you having to explain the matter to me, which I don't doubt you were just about to do."

"Certainly," he said smoothly. "But we have more immediate important matters to discuss. The business of the boy can wait."

"No," Aurora said. "I don't think it can."

Lord Ortolan tutted and stalled, but since he couldn't contradict her command, he eventually called for a footman to show the boy's family into the solar, a more intimate space than the cavernous great hall.

Aurora was glad. She liked the solar. There was no throne for her to sit in, intimidating everyone who came to make a request of her. Instead, she sat in a cushioned chair and considered ways to find the groom. She would alert her castellan and have his soldiers sweep the land. Perhaps once she'd spoken to the family, she'd have more information about how to focus the search.

A few minutes later, three people entered: a man, holding his hat in his hand, and two older women. The man bowed low, and the women sank into deep curtsies.

"Your boy has gone missing?" Aurora asked.

One of the women stepped forward. She was thin enough that she might be blown over by a curl of smoke. A worn shift hung from her gaunt shoulders. "You must convince the faeries to give back our little Simon."

"You believe *faeries* took him?" Aurora said, incredulous. "But why?"

"He had a charmed way with animals," said the man, and Aurora realized he must be Simon's father. "And he could play a reed pipe like no one you ever heard, though he's barely fourteen. Why, even the ancients would be up on their feet and dancing. The Fair Folk are jealous of clever boys like that. They wanted him for themselves."

This was exactly the reason the country needed a treaty, and exactly the reason one was so hard to negotiate.

Aurora was certain that the Fair Folk hadn't taken the boy—faeries were fond of pipers, sure, but not *that* fond of them—and she was equally certain that Simon's family wouldn't believe her without evidence.

"Could something else have happened to him?" she asked gently.

Lord Ortolan cleared his throat. "The boy was a thief."

The second woman spoke. Her hair was white and pinned up into a large bun, and her voice shook a little with anger. "Whatever you've heard—those other stories, they're false."

"Other stories?" Aurora prompted them. "What was he accused of stealing?"

"One of your horses, Your Majesty," said Lord Ortolan. "And a silver dish besides. The reason no one can find him is that he ran off."

"That's not true," said the man. "He was a good boy. He liked his work. He had no sweetheart and he'd never so much as been to the next town."

"I will see what I can discover," Aurora promised.

"The faeries have him," said the elderly woman with the bun. "Mark my words. Your Majesty, pardon my saying so, but they're feeling emboldened with you on the throne. Why, just the other day—"

"The cat," the man said knowingly, nodding.

"Cat?" Aurora asked, and almost instantly regretted the question.

They told her the tale of the storyteller and Maleficent, and though none of them had been present when it happened, Aurora didn't doubt it was true. By the time they were ushered out, some twenty minutes later, Aurora was left with a heavy heart.

"If you will excuse me . . ." she said to Lord Ortolan, and began to rise.

"Your Majesty"—he cleared his throat—"you may recall that there was something I wanted to discuss with you earlier."

"I recall that you didn't want me to talk to Simon's family," she said sharply. Not for the first time, she considered dismissing Lord Ortolan. If only he didn't have so much influence at court. If only he weren't the person who understood how so many things in the kingdom worked. It was clear that King Stefan had allowed Lord Ortolan to manage all the practical aspects of Perceforest while he nursed his obsession with Maleficent and argued with her severed wings.

"I didn't want you to have to waste time speaking with the rabble yourself. After all, it is my duty and privilege to protect you from such things as would naturally bring a young lady discomfort," Lord Ortolan said smoothly. "But there is something else as well."

Aurora thought of the breakfast she hadn't had time to take more than a bite of and all the other things she ought to be doing. She thought of the missing boy and the villagers' report that Maleficent had turned a storyteller into a cat. She thought of the treaty. She didn't want to hear about something else that had gone wrong.

But she couldn't say any of that aloud, especially to Lord Ortolan, who would love to take away all her problems and make all her decisions for her. "Very well," she said instead. "So what is it?"

He cleared his throat. "Flowers, Your Majesty. A wall of flowers is growing, encircling Perceforest."

"That sounds *pretty* . . ." she said, baffled by his grim tone.

Lord Ortolan frowned and went to a desk where a wooden box rested. "Yes, I can see why it might sound that way. But you will recall the wall of briars that surrounded the Moors, protecting it from humans."

Aurora waited for him to explain the significance of the briars. "Is our kingdom cut off from the others? Is trade no longer possible?"

Lord Ortolan cleared his throat again, noisily. "It's not

that—not *exactly*. The roads are clear of flowers—well, the flowers have grown in an arch above the roads. One can still enter and exit Perceforest. But tradespeople are frightened. Many are turning back. And some of our people are afraid to leave for fear the passageways *will* close."

He opened the wooden case. Inside was a length of vine with two large roses attached, both flowers the deep black of spilled ink. The outside of each petal shone like polished leather, while the insides had the thick dull nap of velvet. At the end of each petal was a spike like the stinger on the tip of a scorpion's tail.

"Ah," said Aurora. "I can see how those might be a little alarming."

"A little?" Lord Ortolan choked on the words. "This must be your godmother's doing, but what does she intend?"

"She means no harm to anyone in Perceforest," Aurora said, stroking one of the black petals. It was extraordinarily soft, aside from the stinger, and very beautiful. Just like her godmother.

"Your Majesty, how can we know?" Lord Ortolan insisted.

"She's being *helpful*," Aurora said with a fond smile, "which means it will be much harder to convince her to stop."

4

When Maleficent had placed a crown on Aurora's head, she hadn't thought she was putting Aurora in danger. Making her queen of two kingdoms had seemed like a perfect plan. After all, Aurora had wanted to live in the Moors, and she was already the heir to Perceforest. She was a human the faeries loved, and humans would be predisposed to love her, too.

Maleficent believed she would make a wonderful queen.

And she *was* wonderful.

But the job turned out to be terrible. In the Moors,

the only expectation of Queen Aurora was that she guard them from outside threats. But in Perceforest, danger came from all sides—and so did obligations; when her people didn't want to trick her or cheat her or steal her throne, they wanted her to solve all their problems.

And since Maleficent was the one who had put Aurora in that position, she'd decided to help her—in small ways. Nothing too obvious.

A few seeds planted along the borders. Potions cooked up to guard Aurora against poison. The occasional criminal waking in the royal prisons, begging to confess. Lightning storms drawn from the clouds when it seemed as though Perceforest's farmlands had gone too long without rain.

And if people looked up in fear when thunder crashed around Aurora, well, perhaps that was no bad thing, either. It was a good reminder that if the humans ever thought to move against her, there would be no one to hold Maleficent back.

But in her travels through Perceforest, she discovered something she hadn't expected.

The nature of humans.

Maleficent had known a few of them, of course, but, well, a *vanishing* few. She hadn't really understood how desperate their lives could be. She hadn't seen them digging in the dirt for shriveled vegetables, their faces lined and their bodies bent. She hadn't seen hungry children, or young lovers torn apart by greed, and she hadn't seen the cruelty neighbors inflicted on one another.

Now she alighted in trees and watched. It made her recall watching over Aurora when she was a baby, neglected by the pixies who were supposed to raise her.

It made her think of Stefan, orphaned and desperate for power.

And it made her certain that getting Aurora away from other humans was the best way to keep her safe.

But as much as she might like to, she couldn't just drag the girl back to the Moors and keep her there. No, she had to tempt Aurora to spend more and more time among the faeries until she forgot all about the humans. And for that, Maleficent needed something extraordinary.

A palace in the Moors.

A majestic place that would make the castle in Perceforest appear like a dull pile of rubble.

Stretching out her fingers, she began to twist and shape the earth, conjuring up soil and rocks in a spiraling path up a hill. And then she moved on to the palace itself, smoothing out great boulders into walls and thickening vines into staircases. Spires rose into the air, thick with moss, green and magnificent. When she was done, there was a castle where no castle had been, all of leaves and flowers, wood and stone—a living thing, pulsing with magic.

And if a part of her hoped to make up for the hurt she'd already caused Aurora with a truly extravagant gift, if part of the structure itself felt as though it were shaped from her guilt and her fear of losing Aurora again, well, that only made it more beautiful.

5

Aurora spent the later part of the morning and the early part of the afternoon writing letters and sending pages running to deliver them. She wrote to her castellan, commanding him to send men-at-arms and watchmen to look for the missing groom. She sent another note to her stable master, asking him to provide a description of the boy—and to verify that a horse was missing. And she got a footman to check on the silver dish.

Then she wrote to her godmother.

The other notes could be carried by messengers, but that one could not. Aurora took it up to the dovecote and found a bird she had brought from the Moors. Its wings were white, its head black. Aurora had named it Burr.

"Here you are," she whispered to the bird as she bound the note to its leg with a gently tied loop of twine. Then she took the bird out, holding the fragile body in her hands. Beneath soft feather, she could feel the rapid beat of its heart. "Take my message straight to Maleficent."

When she threw the bird into the air, she thought of other wings. Wings trapped by her father, King Stefan. Wings beating their way home.

By the time she was supposed to go out riding with Count Alain and the rest of the court, she was eager to be in the woods, surrounded by the comforting scents of damp earth and fallen leaves. Yet she wondered if she should cancel the outing. Somewhere in her lands, a boy was missing, and while it was entirely possible that he was riding a stolen horse to another town, she couldn't stop thinking of his family's pleas for her to believe better of him.

But she reminded herself that being a ruler meant not becoming distracted by every problem in her kingdom. She needed to go on the ride, because if she could show her court the beauty of the Moors, they might yield on the treaty.

It wasn't easy to focus on the bigger picture, but she had to try.

Marjory talked her into changing her kirtle, and she put on a heavier one of deepest green with an embroidery of vines around the throat. With it, Aurora pulled on warm stockings, riding boots, and a woolen cloak trimmed in wide ribbons.

Marjory also rebraided her hair into a series of plaits that crisscrossed in the back, like the ribbons of a corset. Then, finally, Aurora was racing down to the stables, cloak flying behind her.

But just as she arrived at the stall where her dappled gray horse, Nettle, waited, she heard a familiar buzzing behind her.

Knotgrass, Thistlewit, and Flittle flew into the stables, obviously out of breath. Although the pixies had worn human guises for most of her childhood, they didn't bother with those now and went almost everywhere carried on their small colorful wings.

"Oh, good, we caught you in time," said Flittle, tugging on her bluebell-shaped hat.

"What's the matter, Aunties?" Aurora asked, alarmed.

"You shouldn't run like that," scolded Knotgrass, wheezing a little. "Elegant ladies do not hurtle through their castles!"

"Nor do they scowl," said Flittle at Aurora's expression.

"And must you ride such a fierce-looking animal?" asked Thistlewit. "It just doesn't seem safe. Isn't there a nice rabbit that could carry you? A silky, gentle rabbit. Doesn't that sound nice?"

"She's too big for a rabbit," said Flittle.

"I could make one larger," said Thistlewit, "or shrink Aurora. Wouldn't you like to be a bit smaller, my darling?"

Aurora, knowing their magic was erratic at the best of times, shook her head vehemently. "I like myself just the size I am. And I like rabbits just the size they are, too. Now, *what* is it that you've come to talk to me about?"

"Oh, just a very little thing," said Flittle. "Sometimes your subjects come to us to ask about your *preferences*. Because of our closeness to you. Why, we think of ourselves as your most *trusted counselors*, and I am sure you would agree."

Aurora knew them well enough to be sure that nothing would make them think otherwise, so she held her tongue.

Knotgrass broke in. "Just the other day, we told the cook all about your favorite dishes. Of course, I told her you love trifle, especially the kind with raspberries. . . ."

Flittle put her hands on her hips. "And I informed Knotgrass that raspberries give you a *rash*."

"Tripe," said Thistlewit.

"Rude!" exclaimed Flittle.

"No," said Thistlewit. "Aurora loved it. I am almost certain. I have a distinct memory—"

"My favorite food is most definitely not *tripe*," said Aurora. "And I haven't gotten a rash from raspberries since I was very small—which I no longer am, although no one seems to realize it."

With that, she swung herself onto her horse's back. And without another word, she rode out to join the courtiers waiting for her in the courtyard.

By the time she got there, she felt guilty. She knew the pixies meant well. She was just tired. And cranky. And overwhelmed.

"My queen!" Count Alain called at her approach. He wore a velvet jerkin. His horse was black, its coat brushed to a high shine. A bow was strapped to the side of his saddle.

Beside him was Lady Fiora, his younger sister, dressed in blush pink. She waved eagerly to Aurora as she approached, and then she turned to say something to Prince Phillip. He was astride a white horse, with a sword at his side. When he looked at Aurora with a half smile on his face, she felt lighter than she had all day.

But before she could ride to him and pour out her troubles, Lord Ortolan drew his horse beside hers.

"What a fine idea of Count Alain's," he told Aurora.

Ahead, Prince Phillip said something to Lady Fiora. Her laugh rang out, and Aurora wanted nothing more than to tell Lord Ortolan to go away. It was only her memory of her rudeness to her aunties that made her bite the inside of her mouth and nod. "Yes. Indeed, I ought to go and thank—"

"You know," Lord Ortolan said in his usual ponderous tones, "I was there when your father took his throne."

King Stefan had done that by slicing the wings from Maleficent's back and presenting them to Aurora's grandfather. Aurora hated to think of it, and she hated the way Lord Ortolan's tone made it sound as though, to him, this was a good memory.

"I was the one," Lord Ortolan went on, "who showed him how to behave like a ruler. You know he grew up very poor, a shepherd's son. Thanks to my tutelage, no one remarked on his humble beginnings. He presented himself as a king, and a king was all anyone saw. I can teach you the same things."

"I am not like my father," said Aurora, and the hardness in her tone surprised her.

"No, but you're clever for a girl," said Lord Ortolan. "You'll learn quickly."

One other thing Aurora hadn't grown up with in the woods: *men*. She hadn't gotten used to being dismissed by them, and she hadn't had to figure out what to do in response.

Oblivious to Aurora's vexation, Lord Ortolan went on. "Things are different for you, of course, being a young lady. The dangers are greater. That is why my advice is invaluable. For example, you may have noticed that Prince Phillip has been dangling after you. I believe he is here to win your land for Ulstead through marriage. Be wary of him."

"Marriage?" Aurora echoed, startled out of her growing anger. "You think Phillip wants to *marry* me? You don't understand—"

"There are some very eligible young men among your own people," Lord Ortolan said. "And once you wed, you will no longer have the burden of ruling. When your father was king, Queen Leila had no matters of state to concern herself with. There are a few nobles that I could recommend. . . ."

For a moment, Aurora understood the temptation Maleficent faced, with all the magic she possessed. If Aurora could have turned Lord Ortolan into a cat, she couldn't swear that she wouldn't have.

"Let me make this clear. *I* am the queen of Perceforest and the Moors, and I do not consider ruling them a burden." She squeezed her legs more tightly against Nettle's sides. The horse sped up, leaving Lord Ortolan and his annoying advice behind.

6

Maleficent paced back and forth across the Moors, the hem of her long black gown sweeping over mossy rocks and loam. The charcoal feathers of her wings fluttered in the wind.

Diaval, in his raven form, pecked at beetles that scuttled along at her feet, their green wings making them appear like scattered jewels.

"She's too sweet-natured," Maleficent said.

There was no reply from the raven.

"Are you listening?" she asked Diaval, scowling. With

a flick of her hand, he became human, crouched on the ground, a beetle still in his mouth.

He got up with a sigh, crunching the bug. His hair was as black as his wings had been, and there was something inhuman in his eyes. It comforted her.

"Always, mistress," he said, wiping a stray leg from his lower lip. "Too sweet-natured, Aurora. Terrible personality flaw, to be sure."

That only deepened her scowl.

"She was raised by *pixies*," Maleficent went on. "In the *woods*. She will fall prey to deception."

"Yes, mistress. Very probably," agreed Diaval.

"Tell me more of what you observed," Maleficent commanded, annoyed by his unwillingness to spar with her.

Nearby, a black cat, who had once been something else entirely, was trying to climb a tree to get at a pigeon perched on the lowest branch. The cat scratched its way up the bark only to slide back down a moment later. The pigeon—the one Aurora called Burr—appeared entirely unconcerned.

"She was out riding," said Diaval. "That boring old wiffle-waffle of an advisor was in Aurora's ear."

"What of the prince?" Maleficent asked.

"Riding with the men-at-arms, perhaps to evade several young ladies attempting to separate him from the herd."

She began to pace again, her brow furrowing. "And the count who invited her?"

"As far as I can tell, they barely spoke a word to each other," Diaval said.

"For now." Maleficent pulled Aurora's note from the folds of her gown and smoothed it out, perusing it once again.

Her gaze fell on the cat. Diaval had found it and persuaded Maleficent to bring it to the Moors, on the theory that it might not know how to do cat things very well yet. It seemed to her, from the way it watched him in raven form, that it was catching on perfectly well.

Her lip curled as her gaze went to the castle and her frustration mounted. "I mislike Aurora being so far away from us. Would it have been so terrible if she'd remained asleep for just a little bit longer?"

"*Mistress*," said Diaval, genuine surprise on his face.

"Only a teensy bit," Maleficent said with a pout. "Until she was twenty-five, perhaps."

Diaval didn't answer, but it was clear that he thought she had gone too far.

Maleficent gave a great sigh. "We will just have to make sure nothing happens to her. Now that the curse is broken, she can be protected and safe. Always."

"Are you speaking of your, uh, *flowers*?" Diaval asked.

The blooms were coming along quite nicely, Maleficent thought. Every week the bushes gained a foot in height, the branches becoming denser, the stinging parts growing ever longer and sharper. Eventually, they would be the size of daggers, long enough to pierce a man's heart. That would keep Perceforest safe, even if—according to her note—Aurora wasn't convinced they were necessary.

Maleficent frowned. "If only she would *terrify* them, fill them with awe and fear. Humans love nothing that does not fill them with fear."

"I'm not afraid of you," he said.

She looked at him for a long moment, not sure she had heard him correctly. "And?"

"Oh, nothing," he continued. "I suppose I'm not human."

"No," said Maleficent, placing her finger under his chin, her sharp nail pressing against his skin. "Nor, as you remind me regularly, would you want to be. Now, do you know what I expect of you?"

He raised a single brow. "One never can be entirely sure, mistress."

"I expect you not to fail me," she said, turning away from him in a sweep of black cloth. She looked over her shoulder. "Or Aurora. Now let us go to her."

Diaval blinked back at Maleficent, something of the bird still in the tilt of his head. "She is not afraid of you, either, you know. She never has been. And she is entirely human."

7

Still fuming, Aurora urged her horse ahead of
Lord Ortolan.

"Was he prosing on?" Lady Fiora asked, falling back
to ride alongside Aurora. She glanced over her shoulder at
the advisor. "The old fossil. I suppose he hopes to bore you
into letting him get control of your treasury."

"He seems more worried Prince Phillip will steal my
heart," Aurora confided with a laugh.

Lady Fiora laughed, too. "No chance of that. He's
returning home to Ulstead."

Aurora wondered if her horse had taken a wrong

step, because she experienced the curious sensation of her stomach dropping. "That's not possible. He would have said something."

Her companion lowered her voice to a whisper. "My maid overheard him talking with a messenger from his kingdom just today. Apparently, he is to depart within the week."

Aurora took a deep breath, drinking in the familiar scents of the forest. The sun dappled the ground, filtering through the leaves and making shifting patterns along the forest floor. It ought to have made her feel better, but all she could think about was Phillip's leaving.

Somehow she'd imagined things would go on exactly the way they were.

But of course, that was impossible. His parents must have missed him. And he had duties back home, perhaps even including an obligation to a marriage, as Lord Ortolan suggested—just not one to her.

"Don't you love it out here?" she forced herself to say, her voice brittle.

Lady Fiora looked around. "I don't mind being in the forest with a large party, but I worry over *sounds*. There could be bears. Or adders. Or faeries."

Aurora considered telling Lady Fiora that bears and snakes would run the other way from all this human noise, but she wasn't sure Lady Fiora would find that at all reassuring.

"The faeries won't hurt you," Aurora attempted.

Lady Fiora gave Aurora a strange look but didn't contradict her. One didn't contradict a queen.

"And there are lots of wonderful things in the woods," Aurora went on, steering her horse toward a wild blackberry patch. She leaned down and plucked a few ripe berries, then held them out to Lady Fiora, who she knew had a sweet tooth. "See?"

Lady Fiora's delicate nose wrinkled. "Uncooked fruit? That's sure to make you ill."

Count Alain rode up beside them, catching sight of the bounty in Aurora's hand.

"How enterprising," he said. "Perhaps we can bring those to the kitchen. I am sure the cook would be charmed."

The palace cook sent up no fruit or vegetable that wasn't thoroughly stewed or braised or baked into a pie. Aurora had previously supposed that was to show off the skills of the kitchen, not that the nobles believed that eating fruits and vegetables raw would do them harm. Aurora had spent her childhood devouring raw berries, often going home with her hands and mouth stained by them, and no harm had come to her.

She popped the blackberries into her mouth, to the astonishment of her companions.

"Someday soon I hope to convince you to visit my family estates," Count Alain said, recovering from the shock. "I can see that you have a great appreciation for the outdoors, and my own little corner of Perceforest is quite rustic."

"You must miss being home," Aurora said to Count Alain, but it was of Phillip she was really thinking.

"And yet it is hard for me to tear myself from your side," he said with a smile. "The only solution is for us to go together. There are rivers choked with fish. Woods ripe with game. And, of course, iron mines—the richest in all Perceforest."

Aurora repressed a shudder. It wasn't Count Alain's fault that his part of the kingdom produced iron, which was poisonous to faeries. Iron was useful in other ways. Pots and wagons and barrels all had iron.

"Those mines are the source of my family's wealth. It has allowed us to construct an estate that I hope will meet with your approval. We have imported orange trees from the south and keep them warm by growing them indoors."

Before Count Alain could go into more detail about the splendors of his estate, Prince Phillip's horse trotted up alongside Aurora's steed.

"I hate to interrupt," Phillip said, "but I think I may

have found a vantage point. We're very close to the place where you were crowned, in the Moors, aren't we?"

She remembered that day, remembered her aunties bringing her the crown and Maleficent declaring her the queen who would unite the two kingdoms. She had taken the bark-covered hand of one of the tree warrior sentinels when she'd noticed Phillip was among the faeries, with his gaze on her and a soft smile on his face. Her heart had beat so hard that she'd felt something a little like panic.

That was before she knew about the kiss.

He's not the one for you, Thistlewit had said later that night. *If he couldn't wake you, then he's not your true love. Such a pretty boy as that, he probably loves himself a little too well to have room to love anyone else.*

At first it had stung to hear that, but later it was a relief. After all, if Phillip didn't love her, then it was okay to tell him embarrassing things. It was okay to be honest. It was okay to be totally herself.

"Yes," Aurora said. "Very close."

"You have been in the Moors before, Prince Phillip?" Lady Fiora asked. "You must be very courageous."

That earned her a swift glare from her brother.

"Not at all," Phillip said. "It's an extraordinary place. There are plants growing there that I've never seen before, roses in colors I don't have the words to name. And everything is alive. Even the rocks move. All the leaves in a tree might take flight and only then would you realize you were in the middle of a swarm of faeries."

Aurora had never heard a human describe the Moors so beautifully.

Lady Fiora was staring at Prince Phillip as though she thought him even braver than before. "I would have fainted if I saw half those things. But I trust you would have caught me."

Aurora rolled her eyes. Prince Phillip looked flummoxed by her flirtation. "I suppose I would have tried."

"If we're so close and you like them so well, perhaps you should explore the Moors again now," Count Alain said testily. "That is, if Aurora will let you."

Phillip laughed. It was a kind laugh—kind enough to draw the sting from Count Alain's words. "Well, I was wondering if we could see into them from up there. Since Aurora brought us all here to get a look." He pointed up the hill. There seemed to be a ledge of stone above them, but it meant riding through an area that was both off the path and thick with fir trees.

Aurora steered her horse up the hill with a mischievous grin. "I believe we can. Let's scout ahead." Phillip followed her.

"Where are you going?" Lady Fiora called after them.

"To see the Faerie Land!" Prince Phillip called back.

Lady Fiora hesitated, looking at her brother. Count Alain glowered.

Aurora saw Lord Ortolan sitting astride his horse and, despite herself, remembered his warning: *He is here to win your land for Ulstead.*

But he wasn't. Phillip was going home. And he hadn't even told her.

He would go back to his own country and eventually marry a noblewoman there. And while they would always be friends, his life would probably grow busier. He would have less time to spare. She would be less and less a part of his life. The more she thought, the more inevitable it seemed, and the more heartsick she grew.

A little way up the hill, Phillip stopped his horse.

Where the Moors began, the landscape changed. Crystal pools of bright blue water washed around tall pillars of stone, and small rocky islets dotted lakes. The trees were wrapped in bright vines of vibrant green. And Aurora could see clouds of what appeared to be butterflies blow across the sky. Wallerbogs scuttled along the banks. Mushroom faeries peeped out at them from behind rocks while water faeries leaped from the depths, their glowing blue bodies shining in the sunlight.

Yes, this would be a perfect spot to bring her court.

"I wish we could leave the other riders and go swimming," Prince Phillip remarked.

Aurora laughed. "Lord Ortolan's heart would stop."

"And we know Lady Fiora would faint," he returned, "especially when I dunked you under a lily pad."

Aurora shoved his shoulder. "You wouldn't dare dunk me!"

"You're free to consider it an act of war from a neighboring kingdom," he said.

She opened her mouth to give some reply when the words struck her. *A neighboring kingdom.* His kingdom.

"Phillip," she began, "is it true—"

But before she could ask, shouts came from the men-at-arms. Phillip and Aurora shared a glance, and then both started back down the hill.

Halfway there, she spotted a raven wheeling through the air. A very familiar raven.

What was Diaval doing?

When she got to the bottom of the hill, she found her men-at-arms surrounding a large bush. Their weapons were drawn.

She thought of the missing boy, Simon. Could he have just gotten lost in the woods?

"Wait!" she cried, jumping down from her horse's back. "Whatever you have trapped there, don't hurt it."

Phillip was beside her in an instant, his sword drawn.

"It's no beast or faerie, Your Majesty," said one of the men-at-arms with a smirk.

Another stuck a pole arm into the bush. A howl went up—a very human howl.

"Stop!" Aurora said. "That's cruel."

The soldiers looked rebellious, apparently unsure whether to obey. After a moment, they drew back from their quarry.

A man crawled out of the bushes, carrying a brace of rabbits close to his chest. He had a scraggly beard, and his ragged clothing hung on him. He looked around at the riding party, staring openmouthed at Aurora, then took off running.

Three soldiers chased him down, one tackling him into the dirt. Then the other two grabbed the man by his arms and forced him up to his knees.

"A poacher," said Lord Ortolan with disgust. "Hunting on the queen's lands, no less."

Lady Fiora was huddled with a few of the other young women, their horses drawn into a knot. They looked a little frightened, and Aurora began to realize that they expected her to punish the man on the spot.

"Your Majesty," he said, clutching the rabbits in his hands anxiously, "please. My family is hungry. The yield on our farm was poor this year and my wife is very sick."

A man-at-arms hit him in the side with his pole arm. "Silence."

Another pulled the rabbits from his hands.

The farmer looked down and spoke no more. He was visibly trembling.

"What punishment does he expect?" Aurora asked Prince Phillip. For the man to be so afraid, it must be very bad indeed.

Lord Ortolan pushed his way to the front, clearly glad to be of use. He spoke before Phillip could. "Blinding would be considered merciful."

Aurora was astonished.

"Have him sewn into the skin of a deer and we will set our dogs on him," said one of the men-at-arms. "That's what your grandfather King Henry would have done." A few of the others laughed.

The man began to weep and beg incoherently.

Were these the same humans who thought the faeries of the Moors were monsters? Did they not see how horrible it was to have so much and not be willing to give anything to someone in need?

Aurora bent down near the farmer. "What is your name?" she asked.

"Hammond, Your Majesty," he managed to get out through his tears. "Oh, please . . ."

She hated the idea of hunting, but Hammond was no more cruel than any fox or owl or other animal that killed to feed its young—and she could no more justify punishing him than one of them. He was only trying to survive. Nobles killed far more than they could eat and had to justify nothing.

"You may take rabbits from my woods so long as your family needs food, Hammond," she said.

She turned to the soldiers and drew herself up. This time when she spoke, she didn't hide her anger or her horror at their treatment of the man. "Give him back the rabbits he caught and let him go."

No soldier hesitated to obey her.

"Surely there must be *some* punishment," Lord Ortolan sputtered, "or peasants will take advantage of you. Your woods will be picked clean."

Aurora wanted to contradict him, but it was probably true that *no rules* around hunting on royal land would result in the forest being emptied, and not necessarily by those in need. "I hereby decree that from now forward, any citizen of Perceforest may take one single rabbit from the queen's woods without punishment. Furthermore, anyone who is hungry may come to the palace and be given a ration of barley for every member of their family."

"The royal treasury cannot possibly sustain that," Lord Ortolan said in a quelling manner.

"If the people are fed, they won't have to steal. And they can pay their taxes." If the treasury could afford to pay for all the confections that were set before the nobles, it could afford grain for families in difficulty, Aurora thought. "*Furthermore*, I proclaim that no one, under any circumstances, shall blind another person or sew them into a deerskin and set dogs on them. Is that understood?"

Hammond bowed over and over again. "Bless you, Your Majesty. You are kindness itself." Then, stumbling over his own feet, with his rabbits once more clutched tight against his chest, he started back toward the village.

The entire hunting party was silent. Aurora was sure they thought she'd made a terrible mistake, but she regretted none of it.

Then Lady Fiora shrieked.

8

Aurora spun around.

"What are *those*?" Count Alain demanded, pointing.

Three wallerbogs stood on a fallen tree, blinking at the human riding party with wide, expressive eyes and snuffling with their trunk-like snouts. The mischievous faeries must have heard the commotion and crept over from the Moors.

They were the size of human toddlers, with frog-like bodies and enormous ears that stuck out from their heads.

"Wallerbogs," Aurora said. "They don't mean any—"

"They're hideous!" said Lady Fiora.

Giggling, one of them chucked a fistful of mud at the girl. It struck her right in the side of her head, spattering across her face. Aurora sucked in a breath.

Prince Phillip covered his mouth. One of the other courtiers began to laugh. It was contagious, spreading to the rest. Only Lord Ortolan was grim-faced.

And Count Alain, whose eyes narrowed.

The wallerbogs pointed, laughing so hard that one of them fell over.

"You've given offense to my sister and I will have satisfaction," Count Alain shouted, riding toward them.

With shouts of glee, the wallerbogs scattered, heading back toward the Moors, their frog-like bodies half hopping.

Count Alain kicked his heels into the sides of his mount, sending his horse galloping hard after them.

"Stop!" Aurora shouted. She ran to Nettle and swung herself onto her horse's back. "Do not follow them into the Moors!"

"I will not stand an insult like that to my sister," he shouted back.

"Don't be a fool," Prince Phillip called out.

She could tell the moment Count Alain crossed into the Moors. He passed one of the enormous stones that marked the boundary, and it seemed as though he dropped into smoke, briefly disappearing from view. When he rode out the other end of the fog, he had an arrow notched in his bow. He trained it on one of the retreating wallerbogs.

Then he let the arrow fly.

One of the large vine-covered trees moved. It towered twenty feet in the air, looming over Count Alain. It had enormous mossy horns of bark and a face like a skull made of wood. A tree sentry, a guardian of the Moors.

The sentry backhanded Count Alain off his horse, sending him flying into one of the shallow pools.

The humans behind Aurora screamed.

The tree man lifted Count Alain into the air. Count Alain's legs kicked wildly.

"No!" Aurora shouted, sliding off her horse and running toward them. She was the queen of the Moors as much as she was the queen of Perceforest. Maleficent had put the crown on her head, and the faeries had to listen to her commands as surely as her human subjects did. "Let him go!"

Too late, she realized her mistake.

The sentry heard her, and its fingers opened immediately, letting Count Alain fall.

Now Aurora was screaming.

Wings beating at the air and mouth curved in a bright,

malicious smile, Maleficent caught Count Alain and held him high above the hunting party.

She looked as terrifying as any legend and twice as beautiful.

Diaval, in raven form, circled above her head. He let out a caw.

"Is this yours?" Maleficent asked Aurora. "You seem to have misplaced it."

"Put me down!" Count Alain shouted, ignoring how she'd saved him from a nasty fall.

"Please," Lady Fiora said, taking Aurora's arm, "my brother was only protecting me."

"That creature attacked first," Lord Ortolan protested.

"The wallerbog?" Prince Phillip asked incredulously.

Lord Ortolan went on. "You saw it. My queen, you must order your—your *godmother* to put him down."

"Human," Maleficent said to Count Alain, her fangs flashing as she spoke, "you shot an arrow in the Moors. There was a time I would have crushed your skull for such an offense. I would have put a curse on you so that if you ever shot another, it would come back and strike you through the heart."

Aurora hated it when her godmother talked about curses. But Alain seemed to realize finally that he was in danger.

"Your pardon, my queen," he said, gritting his teeth. "And your pardon, too, winged lady. Fiora is my only sister, and I am overly protective of her."

"Put him down," Aurora said. "Please."

Maleficent swooped low, making the hunting party cry out in surprise. Then she dropped Count Alain, sending him tumbling a short distance into the ferns and vines of the wood. He looked wet, miserable, and furious.

Aurora had thought it would be a simple thing to make peace between the humans and the faeries. She thought it was only a matter of making them see that they were wrong about each other. But thinking of Simon's family and seeing the look on Count Alain's face, she was no longer sure that the peace her treaty promised was possible.

Nor was she certain anyone wanted it.

"Go back to the castle," Aurora told the hunting party.

"Surely you don't mean to remain in the woods alone," said Lord Ortolan.

She looked up at the winged figure hovering above them. "No, not alone."

9

Aurora was nearly her height, Maleficent noted as they made their way through the Moors. She remembered the tiny flaxen-haired child who had grabbed hold of both of her horns and refused to let go.

The willful girl who had giggled at her scowls.

Who had transmuted her anger into love.

But Aurora was not smiling now.

"Tell me about this wall of flowers," she said, hands on her hips. "*Spiky* flowers. Did you think I wouldn't find out?"

Maleficent gestured airily. "Oh, my dear, it was too big

to be a secret to keep for long. I thought of it as a gift — one I could always magic away if you didn't like it."

"Well, I *don't* like it," Aurora said.

"Only consider," said Maleficent, "your borders are protected with no expense to your treasury. No knights need to patrol. No neighboring kingdom can engage in raids. Even brigands and robbers will quail when they realize there is no great distance they can run without trying to pass through a sinister, yet beautiful, hedge."

Aurora did not appear mollified. "You're trying to protect the kingdom the way you protected the Moors," she said. "You put the crown on my head. You have to talk to me before you do things like this. You may have been the protector of the Moors, but you made me the queen of them, remember?"

"I protected the Moors quite well."

Aurora looked exasperated but changed tack. "What about the storyteller in the market? Is it true you turned him into a cat?"

"Well, it's not *not* true," Maleficent said, a mischievous grin growing despite her best attempts to suppress it. "And just think of the stories he will have to tell now! Why, the more I think about it, the more I'm convinced that I've done him a favor."

"Turn him back," Aurora told her.

"Just as soon as I can find him," Maleficent promised, gesturing to the expanse of moorlands, the foggy pools and hollow trees in which a hundred cats could hide. "I am sure he's around here somewhere."

"And the missing groom?" Aurora asked.

Maleficent shrugged. "Really, I can't be to blame for *everything*. You will have to look elsewhere for the boy. And I hope that after today you see that the humans aren't going to come to love the Moors. They're not like you."

"They didn't even have a chance to see—" Aurora began.

Maleficent snorted. "As though it would have helped."

Aurora gave her a wry smile. "Well, since you will be looking for the cat anyway, you can keep an eye out for the boy, too. Maybe *that* will help."

Maleficent was surprised—and insulted. "I told you we're not to blame. Had one of the Fair Folk stolen him away, I would have heard of it," Maleficent told her. "I hope the humans haven't managed to make you distrustful of us."

"Of course not," Aurora said, hopping along a path of stones half sunk in the water with the ease that came from long practice. "But if you found him, it would do a lot to convince the people of Perceforest that we are all on the same side. What happened today showed the lack of understanding between humans and the faeries. Count Alain thought his sister was being insulted, and etiquette demanded he do something about it."

Maleficent gave her a long look.

"He doesn't see the wallerbogs as we do, as gentle and mischievous beings," Aurora admitted. "But I couldn't help pitying him a little, first to be knocked around by one of the sentinels and then to be saved by you. You had only to fail to intervene and he might have fallen to his death."

"When you put it that way, I do see I made an error," Maleficent drawled.

That made Aurora laugh, as though the words were said in jest. Maleficent had only intervened because she hadn't wanted the tree warrior to be blamed for a human death. Personally, she wouldn't have minded if he had fallen.

The more Maleficent thought about it, the more she was convinced that Aurora had learned all the wrong lessons from her.

Because Aurora had been *wrong* about Maleficent. She wasn't a kindly faerie, no matter how many times Aurora insisted that she was. And at least in the beginning, she'd seen Aurora only as the means through which she would exact her revenge on King Stefan.

It didn't matter that Maleficent helped Diaval get her

milk when she was a baby, or that Maleficent caused some vines to save her when she ran straight off a cliff while chasing a butterfly *right in front* of those oblivious pixies. It didn't matter that things had worked out for the best. It didn't matter that Aurora's goodness had woken something in Maleficent she'd thought was lost forever.

It was still foolish to try to see the best in those who were wicked.

And most humans had those seeds of wickedness in them, just waiting to bloom.

But there was no making the girl believe that she'd been mistaken in trusting Maleficent. And Aurora was likely to make the same mistake again, probably with that floppy-haired prince who was mooning over her or that arrogant count desperately trying to impress her. She was going to trust in their goodness, and they were going to fail her, perhaps even hurt her.

"Stay here, in the Moors," Maleficent said impulsively. "Here, where you're safe. Here, with me."

"But at the palace —" Aurora began. Before she could get the sentence out, Maleficent lifted her hands, and in a swirl of golden light, a mist that had hovered over one particular area cleared and her palace of flowers and greenery was revealed. Its spires seemed to spin up into the sky.

The girl could not fail to be delighted by it.

Aurora gasped, her eyes widening in awe. Her hand went to cover her mouth.

"Now you have another palace," Maleficent said, "one the like of which has never existed before and may never exist again. Come, let's tour it."

"Oh, yes," Aurora said eagerly, everything else momentarily forgotten.

Maleficent followed, watching the girl's skirts billow behind her and smiling. Aurora raced through the flower tunnel. Then she spun around in the great hall, causing a shower of pink petals to fall from the canopy.

When she discovered her bedroom, she stopped to marvel at the columns of twisted tree trunks, at the enormous bed with embroidered blankets stuffed with the spores of dandelions in place of feathers, and to exclaim over her open balconies.

Maleficent could tell she adored the palace. She even allowed herself to feel a little smug.

"It's so beautiful, Godmother," Aurora said once they'd toured the entire place, "and I want to stay here with you. But I cannot. If I don't change the hearts and minds of the humans of Perceforest, nothing else will matter."

"You're their ruler," Maleficent said, "and ours. But

you must decide if you will rule like a faerie or like a human."

"You say that as though there's only one correct answer," Aurora replied, kicking a small pebble that was resting near some steps. It rolled over a few times, then grew little legs and scuttled off.

"Perhaps that's what I believe," said Maleficent.

Aurora took her hand, surprising her. It reminded her again of the sweet child Aurora had been—and, for all her height and the crown on her head, still often was.

"I want the humans and the faeries to see that it's possible to live together fruitfully," Aurora said, "to have love and trust between them, as you and I do."

Willful, Maleficent thought. *Foolish. Good.* But what could she say? Aurora had taught Maleficent gentleness when she'd thought that part of her was lost. Now Aurora believed the world could learn gentleness. It was Maleficent's fault that Aurora didn't understand how unlikely that was. But all she could do now was vow not to let the girl get hurt.

And if that meant hurting someone else instead, Maleficent felt perfectly capable of doing it—*delighted,* even.

10

I t had taken Count Alain's servants more than an hour to get the mud out of his clothing. And no matter how long he soaked in a bath of scented water, he still felt as though the grime of the Moors were caught under his nails and behind his ears.

He was not a man who was used to feeling foolish. Under King Stefan, his father had amassed a large fortune. The king had required large quantities of iron, which their mines could supply in exchange for gold and other favors. Ulstead, too, had been an excellent trading partner. When

Alain had inherited his father's title, it had seemed like a simple thing to retain their wealth, especially with a chit of a girl come to the throne.

In fact, the new queen had seemed like an *opportunity*. But dressed in fresh clothing and presenting himself to Lord Ortolan, Count Alain felt far younger than his twenty-eight years. He was embarrassed and furious, and even more furious because of his embarrassment.

The old advisor's chambers were luxuriant, hung with tapestries and imported silks—a reminder that he had been in power for a very long time, guiding events behind the scenes. Count Alain's own father had dealt favorably with him.

"Have a seat," Lord Ortolan said.

A servant brought in a silver tray containing brown bread and butter, along with a pitcher of cider.

"Once, when you were a mere boy," said the advisor as soon as they were alone, "your father was here at the castle, standing before the bed of a dying King Henry. He would have been chosen as the next king, and had that happened, you would be king now. Do not lose the chance to rule again."

"You should have warned me," Count Alain complained. "I didn't expect that tree monster!"

"You were supposed to charm Aurora," said Lord

Ortolan, settling himself in one of the chairs, "not start a fight."

"Did I not arrange the hunt to please Aurora? Did I not endeavor to have my sister pay her courtesies? I thought this would be a simple task." He stood up, restless, and walked to the window. But even looking down on the courtyard made him remember the feeling of hanging in the air, sure he would die. "Aurora is very innocent. That should have been to my advantage."

"And I primed her to be distrustful of that Prince Phillip," Lord Ortolan said. "Really, it's impossible to think how you failed."

Count Alain turned toward him in scorn. "You did me no favors with your warnings. And they didn't work. All Phillip had to do was ask about the Moors and she was swept into his conversation!" Count Alain threw up his hands.

Lord Ortolan fixed his gaze on the count. "You know the Moorlands exert an influence over her."

"They are more dangerous than I thought," said Count Alain, "and that is saying nothing of that creature who slew King Stefan."

Lord Ortolan did not look particularly impressed by this declaration. "Find a way into Aurora's heart. Marrying her is the only way for you to become king."

Count Alain went back to the chairs and threw himself down into one. "Between Maleficent and Prince Phillip, it seems difficult. I fear I have given her a dislike of me, and it will be no easy work winning her over."

"I have a plan," said Lord Ortolan. "In fact, I have several."

11

That evening, Aurora presided over the banquet table in the great hall while dish after dish was presented. Sweet tarts, crèmes, fishes, and game dressed in savory sauces. She couldn't eat. She thought of Hammond, the poacher, whose family might have starved while the entire palace feasted. And she thought of Simon, who had still not been found. She cut her gaze down the table to where Prince Phillip was talking to several courtiers, telling them a story that made them laugh.

"Is something the matter?" asked Lady Fiora, leaning across the table.

"No," Aurora lied, pushing a bit of rhubarb around her plate.

"You must allow me to apologize," Lady Fiora said. "My brother has always been overprotective. But it was my fault. I shouldn't have insulted those—those—"

"Wallerbogs," Aurora said.

"Yes." Lady Fiora looked relieved. "Please forgive Alain. As fiercely as he defended me, he would defend you, were it your honor he felt was insulted."

Horrified though she'd been by Alain's behavior, Aurora couldn't fault his love for his sister. He obviously cared for her a lot, to throw himself into danger the way he had. That was something she could sympathize with.

"I bear your brother no grudge," Aurora said, "so long as he sees how wrong he was and never does anything like it again." Looking down the table, she caught Count Alain's eye. He raised his glass, and she raised hers in return.

If he's actually sorry, then now is my chance, she thought. *I am going to propose he sit down with the other nobles and explain that he jumped to conclusions and that the Moors are only dangerous to people intending to harm the creatures who live there. Maybe this will turn out to be what we need to finally finish the treaty.*

When she rose from the table, Count Alain came to

her side. She waited for him to apologize so that she could inform him of her request.

"I have a gift for you," he said instead, drawing a carved wooden box from his side. "A small token, for the queen who saved my very life."

A few courtiers had gathered close, clearly admiring him for his gallantry. Several ladies smiled at one another with vicarious enjoyment.

A gift was not an apology. But surely he would say something more once she'd accepted whatever it was he'd brought her. And he must feel very guilty to make a show of bringing her a present.

"This is very kind," she began, "but—"

"Not kindness at all," he said so smoothly that it almost seemed as though he hadn't interrupted her. "Entirely appreciation. Please, look inside. I am eager to know if it pleases you."

With few options that weren't outright insulting to him, Aurora opened the box to indrawn breaths all around.

Resting inside was a huge sapphire the deep blue of her eyes. It hung from a heavy metal chain. Count Alain lifted the necklace and unclasped it. "If I may?"

If she refused, he would be offended. And the courtiers who already admired him would be upset on his behalf. But she wanted to let him know that she could not be bribed. "You may, but you and I must still have a conversation," she said sternly, "about the Moors and the future of Perceforest."

"With pleasure," he told her, his fingers overly warm on her skin as he clasped the sapphire around her throat. The chain rested heavily on her collarbone, and as she lifted a hand to touch it, she recognized the metal.

To Aurora's horror, she realized that he had given her a necklace forged of cold iron.

Late that night, Aurora stood on her balcony, surveying both her kingdoms. She could see the town below her, the Moorlands, and even a little of Ulstead in the distance. A chill breeze ruffled her hair.

As usual, she couldn't sleep.

She hadn't bothered to take off the iron necklace. It felt as heavy as her heart. She no longer believed Count Alain could be convinced to help. Yet she had to find a way forward for her two kingdoms. She had to discover the means to make the people of Perceforest see that the faeries in the Moors were helpful, kind, and clever—even if they were also sometimes hot-tempered or mischievous.

But they weren't *cruel* in the way that humans were. No one on the Moorlands starved when another faerie had food to share. No one made war for gain or counted money as more important than friendship or love. If only the humans could see that, they would realize how fortunate Perceforest would be to have the Fair Folk as allies and friends.

Something fell by Aurora's feet, startling her from her thoughts. She looked down and saw a folded note beside her shoe.

She lifted it and frowned at it. Then she unfolded the paper.

The message was written in an elegant hand and contained a message that sounded a little like a riddle: *If I asked you to go for a walk tomorrow in the gardens, would your answer be the same as the answer to this question?*

She looked up, but the balcony above hers was empty.

Aurora frowned. If Count Alain thought that just because he'd given her one horrifying necklace, she was going to agree to go for a walk with him, he was very much mistaken.

In fact, she meant to send him a message right back. She went inside for a quill and inkpot and was ready to write *NO* on the bottom of the note when she realized that she couldn't.

Because if she said no to the gardens, then the answer to the second question would be no as well, which would mean they *were* the same answer—which meant yes. But she couldn't write that, because if the answer was no to the first part and yes to the second, that meant the answers *weren't* the same after all.

There was only one "correct" way to answer the note. Yes to the walk. Yes to the answers being the same. Yes.

Of course, there were other possible answers. Like setting the page on fire. Or ripping it into tiny pieces and throwing them off the side of her balcony like confetti. That would show Count Alain what she thought of him making his sister do his apologizing for him.

Or she could forget the note entirely. After all, she was the queen. She wasn't obligated to answer every ridiculous piece of litter she came across, especially litter that wasn't even formally addressed to her.

Then there was a sound above her. Prince Phillip looked over the edge, his hair falling around his face. He'd let it grow since he'd arrived in Perceforest, and it was already past his ears. He blinked at the paper in her hand and gave her a slightly embarrassed grin. "I thought you might still be awake."

"*Yes,*" she blurted out. "The answer to the riddle, I mean. That's the only possible answer, which is very rude."

"Very," he agreed cheerfully. "But I hoped it would still be the one you wanted to give." His gaze went to her throat and she could tell the moment he saw Count Alain's sapphire necklace, because his smile faded. "There's something I must tell you. I ought to have said it when we were on the hill, but I waited and then there wasn't time."

Phillip was going to say that he was going back to Ulstead, of course. Suddenly, the air seemed colder than before. She shivered, not entirely from the wind.

"You could tell me now," she said, steeling herself.

He grinned down at her. "I'm not sure you'd like me to shout it off the balcony, though the idea has a certain appeal. Tomorrow is soon enough. Will you walk with me? Just for a few minutes? Would you mind?"

"Let me ask you a riddle instead," Aurora told him, although her heart was no longer in the game. "The answer I give is no, but it means yes. Now what is the question?"

"You're answering a riddle with *another* riddle?" he demanded, mock-affronted.

She should have laughed, but the laugh died in her throat at the thought of the conversation that was coming. Leaving him to puzzle over her words, she went back to her rooms to try to get warm.

And to unclasp Count Alain's necklace from her throat so she could throw it into the fire.

12

Prince Phillip had traveled to Perceforest at his father's request. *Go and meet our neighbor, King Stefan. See if you can interest him in trade. I understand that he needs soldiers for his army and that he possesses a large quantity of gold.*

For his part, Phillip was pleased to be on an adventure. He had never before been in a place where no one knew him and where he was unburdened from all the expectations of being Ulstead's future king. Of course, he had gotten instantly lost in the woods. He'd spent the first night sleeping under the stars and the whole second day wandering.

The trees grew too thick for him to see the horizon and get his bearings. The ground was covered in shallow pools and patches of sucking mud that made the way treacherous for his horse.

And then he'd spotted Aurora in her blue gown, gesturing wildly at nothing as she rehearsed a speech she was intending to give her aunties.

Hopping down from his horse, he'd thought first of getting directions. He was a little worried about being laughed at and very relieved to see another person. But the closer he got, the more fascinated he became. Not just by the roses in her cheeks or the shy sweetness of her smile or the way she seemed to belong to the woods, like some sort of sprite. There was something in her face that spoke of mischief—and kindness.

In Phillip's life, there had been precious little of either.

Aurora had been surprised by him, clearly not thinking there was anyone nearby. She'd startled and slipped. He'd caught her hand before she fell, and at her touch, he'd felt as though he'd been kicked in the chest.

For a moment, he'd been unable to breathe.

So he had remained in Perceforest, through the death of King Stefan. Through Aurora's being crowned and the bright summer's fading into autumn.

He'd remained even though he had been unable to

wake her. He hadn't loved her enough, he knew. They'd only just met.

He hadn't loved her then like he loved her now.

Every few weeks he had gotten another letter from his mother and had sent back excuses. But when the latest one had come directly from the hand of a messenger, he knew he had run out of ways to prolong his visit. He took it from his pocket now, looking it over in the moonlight.

Dear Phillip,

You must return to Ulstead as soon as possible. We know nothing of this young queen except she is a great beauty — which we can readily believe, since we suspect she is the reason for your continued absence. But until you return home and your people are able to see you with their own eyes, wild speculation and strange rumors about your doings and safety will continue to abound. Finish your business — whatever it is — and return to us. You have a duty to your own country.

The letter was signed with his mother's full title and her sigil.

He sighed, crumpled it up, and tossed it toward the fire. He would write back and give her a specific date when he would return. That would mollify her enough that he would be able to stay another week or two, at least.

But eventually he would have to return home.

And before that, he would have to do what he'd been too shy to since he'd been in Perceforest: he would have to speak. He must tell Aurora that he loved her.

Over and over, he thought about the words he planned to say, trying out new phrases and then discarding them, attempting to persuade himself that she wouldn't prefer to be courted by some magical creature or one of the nobles who fell over himself to admire her beauty. He whispered words out loud to the cold sky, stopping halfway through each grandiose speech, hating how absurd he sounded.

"Aurora, if my heart were the moon, then you would be the sun, because the sun makes the moon glow, and I glow with, er, love . . . ?

"My heart is an overfull bucket, waiting to pour itself on you . . . ?

"When I think of you, I feel . . ."

She wouldn't laugh at him. She was too kind for that. She would let him down gently and then he could return home, knowing he had no hope of her. When he saw her again, he would have had time to get used to the idea. And they would remain close, which was no small thing for the monarchs of neighboring kingdoms.

Despite those grim thoughts, he smiled, thinking of

her parting words to him that night: *The answer I give is no, but it means yes. Now what is the question?*

A riddle for a riddle.

He puzzled over it, turning the words in his mind. When it struck him, he felt like a fool. It was the answer to the question he'd asked her immediately before it.

Would you mind?

Will you walk with me? Just for a few minutes? Would you mind?

No, she wouldn't mind. She'd go for the walk with him.

Phillip was still smiling when a horned figure landed at the edge of his balcony.

Maleficent.

Her lips were carmine red, and the angles of her face were slightly too sharp. On her shoulder sat a raven, watching Phillip with black eyes. Behind her, lightning needled across the sky, although there had been no storm on the horizon earlier.

She raised a finger as though to curse him.

"Uh, hello," he said, taking several involuntary steps back, his heart speeding. Despite his knowing that she was Aurora's loving godmother — well, *sort of* her godmother — he still found her frightening. "I am sure you were looking for someone else, but — "

"I overheard you and your sickly love speeches. You did not ask for my permission to court Aurora," Maleficent said, her eyes blazing with suspicion. "Like most faeries, I am a stickler for all the little courtesies. Not to mention easy to offend."

Prince Phillip took a deep breath, trying to quash his fear. Squaring his shoulders, he began. "May I have your permis—"

"You may *not*," she said, interrupting him.

"I thought you liked me," he said with what he hoped was a friendly smile.

"I *do not*," she told him, eyebrows lifting. "Although, most of the time I can barely tell you apart from the others. The only thing that is memorable about you is that you've overstayed your welcome in this kingdom."

"We both love Aurora—" he began.

Maleficent narrowed her eyes at him. "Do not speak to her of this foolishness. Do not declare yourself. And do not cross me, princeling. You would not want me for an enemy."

"Of course not," he said. "But I don't understand what I've done to offend you."

She inclined her head toward him in a way that made him wonder if she was considering spearing him on her horns. "You offend me by behaving as though your fleeting feelings are of some consequence. You intend to fling them at Aurora and leave her pining for you as you return home and forget about her."

"I would never—"

"I know about fickle hearts. I know that a love like yours is weak when set against your ambition."

"You're wrong," he said. "About me and about love."

"Do not test me and I won't test your claims." With a sweep of her cape, she went to the edge of the balcony and hurled herself into the night. Her great wings carried her up toward the moon.

Prince Phillip stood still, drinking in gulps of night air until his heart quieted. Until his breathing became normal again.

Until he realized just what he had to say to Aurora, and it turned out to be nothing like what he had practiced.

13

The next morning, Aurora met with her castellan, a large dark-skinned man with cropped hair and a scar that ran across his cheek, pulling up one corner of his mouth. Everyone called him Smiling John, a name Aurora found sinister, since the allusion was to a badly healed wound. He entered the great hall with two men-at-arms. All three of the soldiers were heavily armored and grim-faced.

"We have some news of the boy, Simon," Smiling John said. "Hugh, give her the report."

A solid wall of a soldier, pale with straw-colored hair,

spoke. "We believe he fell in with a band of brigands."

"Brigands?" Aurora echoed, shocked. "But his father said—"

"It's a sad state of affairs when one's own family don't know the lay of the land," the man continued, "yet all too common. Seems that he liked a bit of dicing and that's how he got into debt. From there, he turned to stealing to make the money. Only a matter of time before he stole from the palace."

"So there is a dish missing?" Aurora asked.

"A large jardiniere," said Hugh.

She thought of Simon's family denying even the possibility he'd been involved in wrongdoing. Believing he'd been taken by faeries. They wouldn't want to believe this.

"So where is he?" Aurora asked. "Thief or not, he's still missing. And he's still very young."

Smiling John shook his head. "We found the stolen horse—which led us to one of the brigands, who was trying to pass it off as his own. He's imprisoned now and claims not to know Simon's whereabouts. Our people are still looking. The boy could be lying low. But there's the more likely possibility that the brigands, once done with him, did *away* with him, if you catch my meaning, Your Majesty."

"Do you think that's what happened?" Aurora demanded.

"No way to know," said the castellan, "until we find him, alive or dead."

Aurora nodded. The day had just begun and already she was weary. "Then do so," she said. "Find him. And soon, before the trail goes cold."

Many more meetings followed.

Three boys had caught a flower faerie in the Moors and were keeping her in a birdcage. They'd been spotted exiting back into Perceforest, and one had gotten cursed with a foxtail and a pair of fox ears. The Fair Folk were demanding the flower faerie be released, and the boy was demanding that his curse be removed. The faerie herself was demanding a seven-year supply of honey for her trouble.

A cow had gotten lost and then wandered home with braided flowers around its neck and a tendency toward producing more cream than milk. The cow's owner wanted to know if something would happen to her if she drank it.

With each new accusation, Aurora felt the treaty unravel further. It was only a matter of time before something truly terrible happened—before blood was shed and the humans and Fair Folk returned to being at war, with her unable to halt it.

Finally, Lord Ortolan gave her one piece of good news. Maleficent's black rose hedges had stopped growing, although they showed no signs of receding. "And they give off a distinct scent. It has been described as musky and not unlike the scent of spoiled plums, with a heady sweetness. Is it dangerous?"

"Let us hope not," Aurora said with a sigh. After the conversation about the brigands, she couldn't help feeling that perhaps Maleficent had had a point about the safety of Perceforest's borders. "Tell me, is there anything we can do to lessen people's fear of faeries?"

Lord Ortolan's eyebrows rose. "I understand that you've grown used to them, but they are not like us. They're not human. They're immortal, with powers we don't understand."

Aurora nodded, not in agreement, but with the understanding that he had no interest in helping. "I think a new approach to the treaty must be taken. I wish to hear from my subjects on their concerns—and superstitions—about the Moors."

Lord Ortolan looked alarmed. "Your Majesty, begging your pardon, such a thing could take many, many days to arrange. Your court, of course, comprises many persons from influential noble houses already who have weighed in on the treaty negotiations, and we have sent drafts to those who have the largest estates and the most riches. But for this, they would have to travel here. And we would have to prepare for their arrival—" He stopped at her expression.

Aurora had had enough. "I have spent enough time in consultation with the nobles," she said. "Now I want to hear from the rest of my people."

"Your kingdom is very large, Your Majesty," Lord Ortolan began.

"Let us start *here*, then," she said, "close to the castle. I wish to speak with farmers and tradespeople. This afternoon."

"This afternoon?" Lord Ortolan repeated faintly.

Aurora smiled at him. "I will have town criers sent out immediately to invite people to the castle. And I will go tell the cooks we will need much in the way of refreshment. Perhaps you can send someone to gather up some of those new black roses? They will make marvelous decorations."

Aurora paused. "But I need to talk to more than just the humans. I will send a message to the Moors that I want to talk to the faeries this evening. I am sure they have fears and superstitions, too."

With that, she left him looking as though he itched to overrule her, perhaps even scold her. But he couldn't, and they both knew it.

By that afternoon, Aurora had grown nervous. As she had hoped, many tradespeople and farmers had been willing to take the small payment she'd offered to make up for a day's work, and were busily eating from the spread of cold meats, bread, and pies she'd provided. She was pleased to see that Hammond, the farmer who had been poaching in her forest, had come, although he stayed at the back of the crowd.

She knew she had to stand up in front of them.

She knew she had to listen to them, even if she didn't like what they had to say.

But if she didn't find a way for the faeries of the Moors and the humans of Perceforest to think of themselves as no longer at war, it wouldn't be long before someone did something so terrible that they were back at each other's throats again—this time permanently.

Aurora walked into the great hall and went to her throne. Gone were the winged gold lions that had once been there; her new one was simple and elegant, cut from a block of marble. As she sat, a hush fell over the villagers. She saw their gazes go to the crown shining on her brow.

"People of Perceforest," she said, "you may know me as the daughter of Queen Leila and King Stefan, but remember that I was raised by my aunties and my godmother, faeries one and all."

She saw the surprise on their faces and wasn't sure if they hadn't believed the tales or were merely astonished to hear Aurora herself confirm them. "Now I am not just your queen, but theirs. The queen of the Moors. And I want all of my subjects to come together. For decades, there has been enmity between the humans and the faeries. Why?"

For a moment there was only silence in that echoing hall.

Then a man stood. "We keep clear of the Moors. Those faeries steal your children, sure as anything."

Aurora saw some grim nodding in the crowd and heard a few murmurs of the missing groom's name. She wanted to tell them what she'd learned from Smiling John, but they had no reason to believe her, at least until Simon was found.

A townswoman with dark skin and green eyes stood up. Aurora recognized her as a worker from the buttery. "They lead you around in circles," she said. "So you can't find your way home even on your own land."

"Or put you under a *curse*," said a young girl with red cheeks and an abundance of curls. As she spoke, she was looking at Aurora as though she expected her to well understand the dangers of being around faeries.

"They aren't all like that," Aurora said, thinking of

how she had said much the same thing about humans to Maleficent—and might have to say something very similar to the rest of the faeries that night.

But the townsfolk and farmers all had heard the story of Aurora's curse; all knew she had indeed pricked her finger on the spinning wheel, knew that only True Love's Kiss had saved her. Some of them might have fought beside King Henry.

"They're greedy," said a boy. "They have treasure in the Moors, and they won't share it with us."

Aurora looked at him sternly, wondering if he had been involved in the kidnapping of the flower faerie, if it was his friend who had been cursed with ears and a tail.

"I'll tell you a story of what happened in my neighbor's house," said a farmer with a scraggly beard. "There was a girl who preferred to gossip with her sisters rather than do her chores. Well, she figured out that if she left out a bit of bread and honey, one of the faeries would milk the cows and gather the eggs and feed the pigs. But one day her brother came upon the food and, not knowing what it was for, ate the bread and honey before the faerie could get it. And do you know what that creature did? Cursed the boy, even though it wasn't his fault! Now any milk curdles as soon as he comes near it. The lad makes good cheese, but it's still a shame."

"The faeries frighten us," said a woman in a stained apron, putting her hand on the man's arm.

"It wasn't always that way," said an elderly woman with a patch over her eye. Her gray hair was pulled back into a bun, and her clothes were homespun. As she stood, the room quieted.

"*Nanny Stoat*," several people whispered.

"When I was a little girl, before King Henry came to the throne, we'd seek out faeries for a blessing when a child was born. Many of us would leave out food—and no silly boy would think to eat an offering placed on a threshold—for the Fair Folk are a hardworking people and bring luck with their favor. Used to be that you'd not dare to deny succor to a stranger for fear of giving offense to the 'shining ones'—for that's what we once called them in those simpler times."

Aurora rose from her carved wood throne and walked to Nanny Stoat.

"What changed?" she asked.

"King Henry led us into a war," she said, "and we forgot. The younger generations only knew the faeries as enemies. And though we have always wanted the same things—enough food in our bellies to be strong, enough warmth in the winter to be hale, and enough leisure to have joy—things are different. The nobles take our best crops and demand taxes besides. And they say they need to do it because they need to protect us from the Moors."

"Let me try to remind you of those days," Aurora said, an idea coming together in her mind. "I want you to be able to meet one another in peace. And get to know one another without fear. I have been preparing a treaty to help create laws—so that you don't have to be afraid of them and they don't have to be afraid of you. . . ."

Aurora spotted Prince Phillip on the other side of the hall, walking down the stairs with a book tucked under his arm. He glanced in her direction but avoided meeting her eyes. There was something in his face she couldn't interpret. Perhaps discomfort.

For the first time, she saw the motley assembly of people in her great hall through the eyes of an outsider. She took in their sunburned faces and mended clothes. Could Phillip think that speaking with them herself wasn't a proper thing for a queen to do? That they were not worth hearing?

No, not Phillip. He couldn't think something so terrible. He wasn't like Lord Ortolan.

Aurora realized that she'd paused long enough for people to notice and forced herself to keep talking. "I will hold a festival for everyone," she said, "two days hence.

We will have dancing and games and food. And we will sign that treaty."

That meant she needed to finish it. And she needed to persuade everyone it was in their best interest to abide by it.

At the mention of a festival, a ripple of excitement had gone through the crowd. A few of the young people clasped one another's hands and began to whisper until they were shushed.

"We *and* the Fair Folk?" Nanny Stout asked. "Together?"

"Yes," said Aurora. "Please come, all of you."

Lots of voices rose then, talking over one another. There were many questions and worries, all of which she tried to address. By the time she left the great hall, she believed most of her people would come, even if it was only out of curiosity. Now she just had to convince the faeries.

And Maleficent.

14

No matter how difficult it was sometimes for Aurora to accept that she, who had never set foot in the palace until a few months before, was now the queen of Perceforest, it was still harder to get used to the idea that she was queen of the Moors. She suspected the Fair Folk found it hard to get used to, too. They were accustomed to following Maleficent, their defender, and if they *did* consider Aurora to be their ruler, it was only because Maleficent had ordered it.

In the Moors, Aurora felt like a little girl.

Especially when she found herself holding up her

skirts and jumping from stone to stone, giggling as she dodged mud from the wallerbogs—including the one that had escaped Count Alain's arrow. Then she was speaking with the enormous tree sentinels and scratching under the jaw of the stone dragon. Mushroom faeries and hedgehog faeries, a little foxkin in a drooping hat, and a hob with grass growing from the top of his head all scampered out of their nests and holes.

Eventually, tired out, she rested on a patch of moss as they gathered around her.

Had these creatures, whom she had thought of as friends, truly stolen away children from Perceforest? Cursed those boys? As comfortable as she felt here, Aurora knew that didn't mean the Moors didn't have secrets. She knew that war had been waged on them and that they had fought back.

"I came here tonight to ask you what you think about humans," she said.

There were a lot of frowns exchanged and some snickering.

"Yes," she said, "I know I *am* a human. But I won't get angry. I promise."

Diaval arrived at that moment, walking out of the shadows with a small wizened faerie called Robin by his side.

"Such a human thing to promise," said Robin, "when

you can no more choose how to feel than a cloud can choose when to rain."

"I will *try* not to get angry," said Aurora.

One of the hedgehog faeries stepped forward, giggling. "I think they want our magic."

"And our rocks," said a water faerie, popping her head from the stream. "They want to slice them up and wear pieces of them on their arms and around their throat. Or melt them and make them into rings and crowns."

"They smell funny," said one of the wallerbogs, which seemed rich, coming from a creature who spent so much time in mud.

"And they're loud," said Balthazar, one of the border guard.

"They get wrinkly fast," said Mr. Chanterelle, a mushroom faerie, "the way fingers do in water. But their faces, too!"

"That's called getting old," Aurora said.

The mushroom faerie nodded, seemingly pleased to be given a name for it.

"They *hate* us," said Robin with a frown. "That's what I dislike about them most."

Aurora sighed. "The humans are afraid. They told me stories about stolen children and curses. Are any of those true?"

There were a few murmurs from around the glen. Diaval gave Robin a knowing look. The little faerie frowned. "Sometimes we come upon a child in the woods, unwanted and uncared for. Infants, even. We might take that child and raise it here in the Moors. Who can blame us for that? And sometimes we find a child who would be better off in the Moors. We might take that child, too."

Aurora couldn't dispute that some children weren't cared for and that some parents weren't kind. But she also knew that faeries might not agree with humans about which children would be better off stolen from their families.

"Sometimes," Aurora allowed. "But what about the other times? And what about the curses?"

"We can't deny that we have cursed humans," said Robin. "We are a tricksy people, and the humans have given us plenty of cause. Do they not hunt us? Do they not try to trick us out of our own magic and steal what is ours? We are the ones who should be afraid. They want all we have and all we are—and they want us dead."

"I am a human and I adore you," Aurora said, kissing Robin on top of his head and making him blush. "I have heard stories that humans and faeries weren't always at odds, that there was a time before King Henry when you lived with mutual respect."

There was some mumbling and some reluctant nodding.

"For the humans that was a very long time ago," Aurora went on, "but it can't be so long for all of you."

"Once, it was different," the water faerie said grudgingly. "Then, if they wanted my rocks, they would trade for them."

"And their children would play with us," said one of the wallerbogs.

"And they would leave us treats," said one of the hedgehog faeries. "And we would leave them presents in return."

"Yes!" said Aurora. "And it can be like that again. I know it can. That's why we're going to have a festival. Games and dancing and feasting, with humans and faeries in attendance. And the treaty, finished and ready to be signed."

The Fair Folk blinked at her with their inhuman eyes. There were a few murmurs around the glen.

"Please," she said. "Please come."

Maleficent swept into the clearing, holding a black cat in her arms. It butted its head against her dark gown. Her long nails swept down its spine, making it purr loudly. "Oh, my dear," she said, "nothing could keep us away."

Her arrival and declaration seemed to signal the

meeting was over. The water faerie slipped back into her pool. The wallerbogs began to squabble with one another. A hedgehog faerie scuttled into a nest to take cover. Robin seated himself on a rock and began to carve the top of a long stick, turning it into a staff.

"Is that the—" Aurora began.

"Your storyteller," Maleficent said, lifting the animal in her arms. "But he seems quite content being a cat. He didn't seem nearly so happy as a human."

"No one is," said Diaval. "A dragon, however? *That* I wouldn't mind doing again."

"Turn him back," Aurora said.

"I warn you," said Maleficent, "I didn't much care for his stories."

"You astonish us," Diaval returned. She gave him a sour but not entirely unamused look.

Maleficent let the cat half jump, half drop from her hands. It gave a yowl as it landed in the grass. Then it sniffed the air, as though it had caught hold of some particularly interesting smell.

Maleficent made a gesture with her hands as though flicking water from them. The cat began to grow, and the fur peeled back from a man dressed in traveling clothes. He looked around in confusion and then horror.

"You—you *nightmare!*" he said to Maleficent.

She gave him a wide smile, clearly delighted by his distress. "What a lovely thing to say! Now, mind, don't annoy me again or there's no telling what I might do. Perhaps you might like to try being a fish this time."

Aurora knelt down beside him. "No, no, there's nothing to worry about. She's not really like that." She slid a ring—gold, with a pearl—off her finger. "Here, take this for your troubles."

Maleficent was obviously offended. "I am absolutely *like that*," she muttered.

"Why don't I show him the way out of the Moors?" interrupted Diaval, slinging an arm around the man's shoulder and ignoring his attempt to pull free. "We can commiserate about being transformed. Come along now. There are so few people who really understand our troubles."

Maleficent watched them go, then went to Aurora's side. "Are you pleased?"

"Yes," Aurora said, leaning her head against Maleficent's shoulder.

The faerie absently stroked her golden hair, and Aurora sighed. "Do you think that I would have turned out horrible if I was raised in the palace? Would *I* have hated faeries?"

"I think you were born with a generous heart,"

Maleficent said, "and no one could have made you otherwise."

"Would I have been frightened, then?" Aurora continued, thinking of the girls her own age who had been among the townsfolk and the farmers.

"You were never afraid of anything. Even when you ought to have been."

Aurora gave Maleficent a fond smile.

"Come," her godmother said. "Eat with me."

They dined inside the conjured palace of vines and moss, at a table of gnarled wood. Stacks of honey cakes, a pitcher of cream Aurora hoped wasn't stolen, and duck eggs were all spread out on dishes and bowls of black clay.

When Aurora was full, she lay on her back on mossy cushions and looked up at the stars through a screen of vines.

"You must like this place," Maleficent said, lifting a single brow, "a little."

"Of course I do," Aurora said, stretching out her arms. "I love it. And I love that you made it for me."

Everything felt like it had before Aurora discovered whose daughter she was, what Maleficent had done, and what had been done to her.

She slanted a look at her godmother, who had come to rest on another cushion. She was different with wings.

She took up more space yet also seemed to have a new lightness in her. Aurora had never realized how confined she must have felt, being forced to walk on the ground as Aurora did.

There were many things she hadn't realized.

What had it been like to be so disastrously in love with Stefan and so horrifically betrayed? What had it been like to face him down? What was it like now, to try to trust humans enough to make a treaty with them?

Aurora thought of the meeting she'd had with the villagers that afternoon and Phillip's strange expression. This was the day they were meant to go walking, but he'd never appeared to escort her out, so perhaps he was displeased in some way? The thought bothered her more than it should. She wished she could ask for Maleficent's advice, but she was pretty sure she knew what her suggestion would be.

Cook his heart over a spit. Roast it well. Then discard it.

"Would you like me to make up your bed for you, as I used to when you were a child, beastie?" asked Maleficent.

Aurora grinned at the old nickname. "Yes." It would be good to be away from the Perceforest castle, away from the smoke and the iron and the constant feeling that someone was waiting to corner her.

When she was younger, she had slept in a spider-silk

hammock hung from the branches of an enormous tree. But that night she had a magical bed in a leafy bower.

Aurora climbed in, under piles of blankets of faerie workmanship, each one almost impossibly warm and light.

But a few hours later, while Maleficent dozed on a divan, wings folded as tightly against her back as a bird's, Aurora was still wide-awake.

She willed herself to rest, but as her eyes drifted closed, her whole body jerked awake in nameless terror. After several attempts, her heart was beating so wildly that she knew sleep wasn't coming. And if she wasn't careful, Maleficent might discover her trouble. Aurora knew it would make Maleficent feel awful. Aurora wanted that least of anything.

As quietly as she could, she slid from the bed. She didn't bother looking around for her shoes or even pulling on her overdress. She hurried down the stairs and out of the palace. The moss under her feet was soft and cool and a little damp. The breeze was warm. She began to walk. In the starlight, gems shimmered beneath the waves. She saw wallerbogs snoring gently, sleeping beneath blankets of mounded leaves.

On she went, until she was almost at the edge of the area where there had once been a barrier between the Moors and the human lands. There she heard a sound, too large for a possum and too tentative for a bear. At first she thought it might be a deer come to nibble at the new green leaves.

By the time she realized it was a human, he was too close for it to matter if she screamed.

15

Maleficent wasn't sure what had woken her. She turned to one side on the divan, her gaze going automatically to check on Aurora.

Except the girl wasn't in her bed.

The embroidered blankets were piled up where Aurora ought to have been, one of them trailing on the floor as though she'd kicked her way free of it. Maleficent sat up and looked around. The wind blew through the trees on the balcony, sending down a shower of silvery leaves.

Maleficent walked until she spotted footprints in the

moss. They looked leisurely, unrushed. No doubt the girl would be back in a moment.

But a moment passed, and then another, and Maleficent couldn't help worrying. She began to walk along the path of the footprints, her worry deepening as she realized that they went farther than could have been explained by the needs of a body.

Her wings flexed, opening and closing restlessly with her desire to fly and survey the landscape for Aurora, but her view of the ground would be obscured by thick vines and flowering trees, and she worried she might not be able to pick up the trail easily again once she abandoned it.

Then Maleficent heard a voice. Not Aurora's—a deeper voice, one that might belong to a man. She rushed forward, moving swiftly between trees. She stopped at the sight of Phillip walking at Aurora's side with his hands clasped behind his back.

Phillip, *here*, after she'd warned him. Phillip, defying her.

Maleficent felt a wash of rage so overwhelming that it staggered her, overwhelming even her relief at finding Aurora unharmed. When she looked at Prince Phillip, all she could see was Stefan, and when she looked at Aurora, all she could see was heartbreak.

"You really came here for our walk?" the girl asked him.

Maleficent stepped behind a tree, hiding herself from view.

"I hoped to arrive a bit earlier, but—" He broke off and gave a self-deprecating laugh. "I got lost again. Did you know there are faeries that lead you around in circles? But I spoke to them kindly, and they brought me to you when they were done with their game."

Aurora smiled at him with shining eyes, as though his being a fool were somehow to his credit.

Maleficent ought to have told those faeries who'd been leading Phillip in circles to take him to a swamp it would take weeks to escape. Months, even.

Angrily, she watched as Phillip took Aurora's hand. "I had to see you. I—"

"You're going to say that you must return to Ulstead," Aurora told him, her gaze on their joined hands.

He raised his brows in surprise.

"Lady Fiora told me that a messenger had come from your family." She took a breath and then spoke quickly, as though she'd rehearsed the words and now was just trying to get them out. "I know you must go, but I—I hoped you might be willing to stay a few more days. I am holding a festival, and if you will come and dance with the Fair Folk, surely it will help the people of Perceforest be less afraid of them."

"And if I dance with you?" he asked.

Aurora laughed. "Then I am likely to step on your feet."

"I will wear my heaviest boots," Prince Phillip said.

She looked up into his face. "So you agree to stay a little longer?"

Maleficent began to hope that perhaps she'd convinced Phillip to withdraw after all. Perhaps he really was returning to Ulstead, and he only intended to bid her farewell. Another day or two didn't matter, so long as he was gone.

"There is something more I would say to you," Phillip said. "Before I go, I wanted to tell you —"

No, absolutely *not*.

She ought to have known better. Of course that feckless boy would attempt to take her heart and then swan off to Ulstead, never to return. Of course he wanted Aurora to believe that his love for her would make him less of all the things that all greedy princes are — selfish and power hungry and cruel. But it would be a lie. All of it, lies.

Well, Maleficent would not allow that to happen.

She stepped out of the shadows and walked across the grass, her wings like a cloak spread behind her. She pointed her index finger at Phillip, the nail clawlike in the moonlight. Magic sparked green around her hands. "You disobeyed me, little prince."

Aurora sucked in a breath in surprise. "Godmother! What are you doing here?"

"Interrupting him before he makes a terrible mistake," Maleficent said.

Aurora moved between her and the prince, looking mutinous. "Stop trying to frighten Phillip! What mistake could you possibly mean?"

Maleficent found herself powerless to answer. She couldn't reveal to Aurora she'd overheard his confessions of love; that was the exact thing she didn't want her to know.

"He does not have my permission to be here in the Moors," she said instead. "I have warned him already and do not like disobedience."

"He wished to speak with me," Aurora said. "And he's my friend. And he doesn't need *your* permission so long as he has mine, since *you* made me the queen here."

Maleficent ignored that, too angry to be reasonable. "If his mistake is coming here, yours is to trust so easily. What do you know of him?"

"I never intended to harm Aurora," Phillip said, "or anyone in the Moors. I would swear to it, on my life."

"Rash words." They were a temptation spread out before her like a banquet. *Curse him,* she thought. *Make his promise a living thing. Curse him so that if he causes Aurora the slightest pain, he will feel it three times over. Curse him so that if he raises a hand to a faerie, he will drop dead on the spot.*

"Stop looking at him like that!" Aurora was trembling with rage. Aurora, who hated to get angry. The last time she had shouted at Maleficent, it was because she'd discovered how many secrets were being kept from her. She'd discovered that Maleficent wasn't her protector, wasn't her godmother, but her enemy.

Maleficent never wanted to be thought of as her enemy again.

She took a breath and then another, letting the green magic fade away from her fingers.

No, she would find another way.

"Perhaps it *would* behoove me to get to know Phillip a little better," she said, although she could barely bring herself to look at him with anything other than hostility. But it was Aurora who needed to know him better, to see through his deceptions. And perhaps there was a way to trick the prince into behaving like the person he doubtless was back in Ulstead. "Come dine here in the Moors with us, tomorrow evening. Before Aurora's festival and your departure."

"It would be a pleasure," Prince Phillip said, as though the invitation were a perfectly normal one and not a gauntlet of challenge thrown down between them.

Good. Let him come to the Moors. Let him sit at her

table and eat from her plates. He had no more love for the faeries than any of the rest of the humans. He would be frightened, and once he was, he would show Aurora his true nature.

"You need not," Aurora said, her voice holding a clear desire to warn him off more firmly.

"If he wishes for my approval, he will accept my invitation."

"Oh," said Phillip with a bow, "I never thought to refuse it."

Aurora's eyebrows knitted, but all she said was "Good night, then. It was very good of you to come all the way here to give me your news. I am sorry we didn't get to finish our walk."

"After dinner tomorrow, perhaps," he said.

Aurora's smile bloomed, bright as any star. Maleficent refrained from rolling her eyes.

With a careless wave, Prince Phillip departed the Moors, followed only by Maleficent's steady scowl.

"Why are you determined not to like him?" Aurora asked, whirling on her, a fresh light of anger in her eyes. "He has been a kind friend to me since I was crowned queen. You can't believe he's here to win my hand like Lord Ortolan presumes. And even if you did, you must know that I am uninterested in any courtship!"

"I only wish for you not to make the mistakes I made," Maleficent said, putting a hand on Aurora's shoulder. Perhaps she had acted too much in haste. "You know little of the world, as I once did. I suffered for that lack. I would not for anything wish you to suffer. I would not wish for you to be betrayed, your heart broken—even by a kind friend."

Aurora pulled away. "What am I to do instead? Surround it with thorns, as you did?"

"You are my heart," Maleficent said softly. "And you are right that I guard it fiercely."

16

"Did you hear her this afternoon?" Lord Ortolan demanded, pacing his chamber. "We must act, and swiftly."

He had wormed his way into King Henry's court many years before. He knew how to flatter a ruler, how to inflame ambition in his breast.

It had been easy to steer King Henry toward greater and greater excess, until war with the Moors had been the only way to enrich his treasury. King Stefan had been more difficult, especially after the death of Queen Leila, when he spent more and more time alone, shouting at the pair of wings he'd caged, as though they were likely to give him advice.

But that setback had led Lord Ortolan to greater opportunities. After all, if King Stefan wasn't capable of dealing with matters of trade and taxes, then someone else had to do it. Someone had to note down into official record the gold and silver that was moving through the treasury. And someone had to help those nobles who sought Stefan's favor find his ear. If Lord Ortolan had managed to enrich himself through all that, well, it was only what he deserved.

But none of his tactics seemed to be working with Aurora. She seemed to care little for flattery, and while she had ambition, it wasn't the kind Lord Ortolan found useful to exploit.

"I did hear her," Count Alain said, sitting in a chair. "I don't think Queen Aurora cares a whit for your advice."

Lord Ortolan turned toward him, unable to hide his anger. Count Alain's father had been an easy man to work with. He had understood what it took to accomplish things, and Lord Ortolan had assumed his son would be cut from the same cloth. So far, he'd had cause to regret that. Count Alain was entirely too used to having his own way without working for it. "Be careful," Lord Ortolan warned. "You need me. Not the other way around."

"Oh?" asked Alain. "And I suppose you have another way to get your nephew appointed as your replacement despite being barely older than Aurora herself."

Lord Ortolan gritted his teeth but didn't snap at the count. Alain might be proud and lazy, but he wasn't wrong. And Lord Ortolan was depending on that laziness; otherwise, how would his nephew manage to take over the operation of siphoning funds from the treasury? "And yet you have even less influence than I, even after your extravagant present."

Count Alain sighed. "You said she would be tractable."

"I was wrong. I did not realize how deep the rot ran." Lord Ortolan looked down at the count. "But there is still hope. You will become the girl's hero."

"And just how am I supposed to do that?" Alain complained.

"We need a story. And a villain. And we must separate her from Maleficent and Phillip both," declared Lord Ortolan. "The only question is whether you have the courage to do what must be done."

17

The next day was full of preparations for the festival. The cooks had to bring in enormous wheels of cheese, sausages, barrels of apples, baskets of eggs, and carts filled with sacks of flour, along with scores of promising young people to help them turn those supplies into a banquet.

Fun meant work, and a lot of it.

Maypoles were being erected, ribbons braided, tents sewn, and chairs cut. Musicians were arriving early, having been called from the countryside. Stewpots were being borrowed and spits constructed by the castle blacksmith.

Everyone seemed full of fresh energy. The courtiers were eager to plan their outfits. Two young girls recently arrived from a barony were nearly ecstatic with glee.

"Oh!" said Lady Sabine. She had deep bronze skin and wore her sleek black hair pulled back into a wimple. "We are so terribly excited to be here at court."

"And we did so hope you would give a ball!" said her twin, Lady Sybil. "So it is wondrous that we came just in time for the festival. And there will be dancing, so it is very like a ball, really."

"I suppose it is," Aurora said hesitantly. Everything she'd heard of balls made them sound full of fancy people in enormous gowns. Not like her festival, where everyone would be welcome.

And of course, she was worried about the treaty. She'd listened to everything both the humans and the faeries had said to her and rewritten it herself. She wasn't sure it would make anyone happy, but she hoped it was fair enough that everyone would at least be equally unhappy.

"I hope you will forgive me for saying so, but King Stefan and Queen Leila were quite *dour* rulers," said Lady Sabine. "There's nothing wrong with that, of course, but you are so young that we hoped—"

Sybil jumped in, half like she was talking over her sister and half like they were speaking with one voice and few pauses. "We imagined meeting you so many times. We thought you might be lonely, growing up as you did. And we thought that perhaps you would like to do fun things."

Aurora wanted to say that she hadn't been lonely—not with her aunties and Diaval and her godmother—but that wasn't entirely true. She hadn't had a playmate her own age. She hadn't had anyone to engage in games with and confide her secrets to, at least not until—

She pushed that thought away. "I *hope* we will have fun," she said as Lady Fiora walked up, clearly overhearing the conversation.

"Since you're planning on dancing," Lady Fiora said, "have you thought who you will have lead you out to open the festivities? Someone must bring you out onto the floor."

Aurora hadn't considered that.

Lady Sybil giggled. "Yes, everyone will want your hand, and everyone will be watching to see who you choose. That's so terribly exciting."

"You should dance with Prince Phillip," said Lady Sabine. "He's very handsome, don't you think?"

"Oh, yes," said her sister. "And a prince, so his rank is second only to yours. Perhaps Ulstead would even be offended if you didn't give him the first dance. After all, no one else can claim quite so much consequence."

Aurora thought of his resolution to wear heavy shoes so that she could tread on his feet as much as she liked, and smiled. If she could open the dancing with him, she could relax. He would guide her through the steps without judging her for not knowing them even half as well as any other girl from one of the noble houses would have.

"I suppose I could dance with him if it's the polite thing to do," she said, hoping it wasn't obvious what a relief that would be.

But Lady Fiora looked uncertain. "It might seem as though you prefer him to your other suitors," she said.

"Suitors?" Aurora echoed. "No, no, he's leaving for Ulstead, as you yourself told me."

For a moment, she couldn't help thinking about the night before and his nervousness. He'd wanted to tell her something even after finding out she knew about his going back to Ulstead. And as he'd begun to speak, before her godmother arrived, she'd been afraid that maybe he was going to tell her about something awful. Something worse than leaving. What if he anticipated being busy with his studies and wanted to warn her that he would no longer have time for her? What if he no longer even wished to keep her as a distant friend?

Perhaps Maleficent was right to worry. If the thought

of losing friendship was this painful, losing love must be terrible.

Lady Sybil looked as disappointed as Aurora felt. "I suppose you could choose an elder statesman. Dancing with someone like that could offend no one, but it does seem very dull."

Opening the dancing with someone like the fusty Lord Ortolan would be awful.

"Perhaps I just shouldn't dance at all," Aurora said, but the girls immediately disabused her of that notion.

"Oh, you must dance!" Lady Sybil said. "If you don't, it will be as though you're saying you don't approve of it. No one will dance if you don't."

"I think my brother could be helpful," said Lady Fiora. "Surely no one would think it was exceptional if you walked out with someone from your own land, someone whose family has been loyal for so long. And you know he's the height of elegance."

Aurora thought of the cold iron necklace. "I don't think—" At that moment, her aunts flew into the room in their colorful bright gowns.

"Aurora!" said Knotgrass. "We would like your thoughts on some garlands."

"Yes," said Thistlewit. "I prefer daisies, but—"

"Bluebells would be better," said Flittle.

"Everyone likes peonies," insisted Knotgrass.

"So you see, my dear," said Thistlewit, "you must decide. We wish to drape your festival in flowers. Though it will be hard work to conjure so many petals, you know there's nothing we won't do for your happiness."

"Well, very little," said Flittle.

"Only a few things," Knotgrass put in.

Aurora grinned at them as they bickered. They could be silly and sometimes selfish, but they were always also her own dear aunts. "All those flowers are lovely. Let's have all of them!"

"Delightful!" said Knotgrass. "But are you sure you wouldn't prefer just peonies?"

Lady Sabine and Lady Sybil stared at the pixies hovering in place by the buzzing of their bright wings. They appeared thrilled to meet Aurora's aunts.

"We were just discussing my first partner for the dancing," said Aurora to Flittle. "Who do you think it ought to be, Auntie?"

"As I was saying—" began Lady Fiora, frowning.

"A contest!" said Flittle. "Let someone win your hand."

Lady Sybil and Lady Sabine began praising the little faerie's ingenuity. Flittle appeared immensely flattered by the attention, while the other two pixies grew more and more annoyed.

"I might have said the same thing," said Knotgrass.

"You didn't, though, did you?" teased Thistlewit.

Lady Fiora looked speculative. "I suppose . . . no one could be offended if we have a contest among your people for the honor of leading you onto the floor for the first dance. And you did say you wanted games, my queen."

There really could be no objection to that, Aurora thought. It might even be fun.

"It's brilliant," she said, giving Flittle a hug, surprising the faerie. "Now we've only to think of what sort of contest we should have."

"Not a game of chance," said Lady Sybil. "Too *chancy*."

"A riddle contest," Aurora declared. A contest of cleverness would please the faeries—and if she had any other reason for choosing that particular skill, she never would have admitted it, even to herself.

The twins clapped their hands, delighted.

"Perfect," said Lady Sabine. "Now it's just a question of when to hold it!"

"*Now*, of course," said Lady Fiora. "Why not? We can assemble all the likely gentlemen. It will be a good game to while away the afternoon."

But the more Aurora considered that, the more she disliked the idea of the Fair Folk and the villagers being excluded. "The riddle contest should be part of the festival itself," she said. "Peasant or noble, faerie or human, anyone with the will and the wit can open the dancing with me."

Lady Fiora looked appalled. "B-but you could wind up standing up with someone loathsome. Or filthy. Or who reeks of onion and cabbages." She held her pretty little nose.

"So long as they're very good at riddles," Aurora agreed, "and don't mind my stepping on their toes."

18

The night before the festival, Phillip set off for the Moors on horseback to dine with the faeries.

When Aurora had claimed she knew what he wanted to tell her, his heart had stuttered. Then she'd declared his news was that he was leaving Ulstead. He ought to have corrected her. But he hadn't. He had let her believe that was the reason he had come to the Moors and had asked her to walk with him. It had seemed harmless. He had told himself he would be able to confess his love anyway, just a bit later. And the words were on the tip of his tongue as Maleficent had arrived.

This time, he knew he had to spit them out.

Through the woods he rode, the moon high in the sky. In time the foliage grew dense, the air became thick with the sweet scents of flowers, and the ground filled up with pools of water, reflecting the stars.

A few moments later, small glowing faeries descended on him, flitting around his head and giggling.

"This way," they said. "Our mistress sent us to lead you."

Phillip thought of the last time he had been led by some of the Fair Folk—led *astray*—and he checked the stars. He didn't want to get lost and arrive late, especially not that night. He was well aware that this was a test, and not one he could afford to fail if he didn't want Maleficent to continue to think ill of him. He hoped for her approval, but he would settle for her not threatening him anymore.

It seemed that the little faeries were leading him in the right direction, however. Soon the shallow pools opened into a lake dotted with tiny islands, with lights blooming beneath the surface of the water. Glowing nymphs emerged, surfacing and then diving again, leading him to the largest and most central island, where he could see the outlines of Maleficent and Aurora. A green castle with spires reaching into the sky towered behind them. They stood under a tree hung with glowing lanterns that was beside a long table. Next to them was a collection of faeries, none of their shapes familiar.

Phillip blinked in surprise at the enormous leafy palace. He was absolutely certain it hadn't been there before. But the Moors were changeable and he supposed magic meant the landscape could alter itself in accordance with the whims of the faeries.

As he got closer, his heart thudded faster. If any of the people he knew in Ulstead had seen him doing this, they would have thought he'd run mad. Half the nobles in Perceforest would agree. There were countless stories of faerie food and how even a single bite could bind you to them, trapping you in their clutches forever. Yet with Aurora's shy smile coming into view, he could not regret coming.

If it meant being bound to her, it could not be so terrible a fate.

Aurora wore a flowing dress of pale ivory, which blew in the slight breeze. Her hair was loose and fell around her shoulders in a river of gold, with a garland of flowers at her brow in place of a crown. She looked so beautiful that for a moment he felt as though every other thought had been struck from his head.

"Hello, Phillip," Aurora said, walking down the hill in her bare feet.

She petted his horse's nose, laughing as it snuffled in her hand.

Watching her, he had a feeling of such intense love that it was not unlike agony.

"You look well tonight," he said, and immediately felt like a fool. Surely he knew how to pay her a better compliment than that.

One of the hedgehog faeries came and took the reins of his horse. He jumped down, his polished boots immediately sinking in the mud. He looked down at them sadly.

He was wearing a doublet of the darkest blue velvet, with a bit of golden rope across the chest and at the shoulders. And muddy boots.

Maleficent walked to the edge of the isle, the feathers of her wings ruffling in the wind. Her hair was hidden under her black cap, and there were jet cuffs at the bases of her horns and a necklace of jet beads around her throat. Or at least he thought they were jet beads. Upon second look, they appeared to be shimmering black beetles. When she saw him, her lips stretched into a wide smile—perhaps slightly too wide for Phillip's comfort.

Beside her were Diaval, the raven-man, and a host of other Fair Folk—wallerbogs, tree sentinels, mushroom faeries, pixies, hobs, and foxkin—some which loomed and others which scampered. They all stared at him with eyes that seemed more animal than human.

"You came," Maleficent said, as though that was a surprise to her, and not necessarily a good one.

Phillip offered his arm to Aurora. She took it, her body a warm and steadying presence as he moved away from the embankment and toward Maleficent.

"Godmother," Aurora said, "shall we sit?"

Phillip's gaze went to the banquet table. Along the vast length of it, a scarlet cloth was draped. Plates of silver at various heights were piled with food, some of it familiar, but much of it not. There were heavy pitchers, black glass goblets, and clusters of fat candles, their wax running over their sides to clot in pearls and runnels.

"Yes, of course," Maleficent said, her hand stretching toward the table in invitation. "I wouldn't want either of you to go hungry."

The faerie took her place in an ominous chair at the head of the table. It was tall and had what looked like horns that curved in and then out, carved from ebonized wood. She gestured to the other end of the table, where a matching chair rested. "As the guest of honor, you shall have that one, Phillip. And you, my dear," she said to Aurora, "can be seated at my side."

A possum faerie wearing a cape pulled out Aurora's

chair. It was carved in the shape of spread wings and gilded so that it shone almost as brightly as her locks.

Other faeries began to scamper to the table and find themselves places; some climbed up onto stools, others onto piles of pillows, and a few of the taller faeries sat on low seats made from hollow logs.

At the far end of the table, Phillip considered what Maleficent had in store for him. Even the tableware was alarming. He had what appeared to be a small silver pitchfork on one side of his pewter plate and a dagger on the other. He lifted the dagger experimentally and found it heavy in his hand, the way a real weapon would be.

A small hedgehog faerie poured elderflower water into a black glass goblet in front of him. It perfumed the air with a scent so pleasant that he allowed himself a sip.

It tasted like sweet, pure water, the kind that bubbled up from springs. He guzzled it all in what felt like a single swallow.

This won't be so bad, he thought a moment before he noticed that one of the dishes was creeping toward him on crab legs. He startled, rocking back in his chair.

"Something the matter?" Maleficent called down the table.

"N-no!" Phillip said as another plate scuttled around on the table, veering toward what appeared to be a woman made entirely of roots and greenery. Fat globes of grapes bounced toward him, followed by a dish of mushrooms—chanterelles, chicken-of-the-woods, faerie ring champignon, wood ears, and honey fungus, all cooked with wild garlic leaves. Then marsh samphire, sautéed. A collection of hard-boiled eggs paraded before him next— snake eggs, starling eggs, quail eggs, white and brown, some speckled and some blue. A few plates were carried on the backs of beetles, while others rested on the backs of turtles. Others appeared enchanted to move on their own.

Then a pile of blackberries and damson plums wriggled forward, beside a pot of fresh cream.

Behind it was a plate of crispy fried spiders and a tray of oblong white snake eggs.

A large tureen on wheels was being pulled down the table by a tiny faerie. It contained a bright green potage of wild leek and nettle. The faerie waved around a ladle in a slightly threatening manner and then dumped some of the soup unceremoniously in a bowl in front of Prince Phillip.

"We hope you don't mind simple fare," Maleficent said with a wide, malicious smile.

Beside her, Aurora had an uneasy expression. She was looking at Phillip as though she fully expected him to flee the table. And he had to admit that he was tempted. In the air overhead, what he at first had taken for oil lamps suspended in the trees turned out to be more tiny faeries, glowing with pale yellow light and peering down at him.

He thought of a story he'd heard from his nurse when he was a child, about a girl who was sent by her wicked stepmother out into the cold to die. In the snow, the girl stumbled on a witch sitting by a fire. The girl was so polite that the witch gave her a warm fur coat so that she passed the night cozily. When the girl returned home, she discovered her pockets were laden with treasure. Jealous, the stepmother sent her own daughter out into the cold the following night. But her daughter was rude to the witch, so the witch put out the fire and let that girl freeze to death.

He knew that faeries hated many things, but above all, even more than iron, they hated uncivility.

"This all looks delicious," Phillip said, somewhat unconvincingly, even to his own ears.

"Try something," Maleficent said, bringing a black grape to her mouth and biting into it. The moonlight caught on her fangs, making them unmistakable. "I wasn't sure what you liked, so we cooked up a little of everything."

"Yes, I can see that," Phillip said, looking at the vast number of mysterious dishes in front of him.

Aurora had a blue egg on her plate, along with some berries and a cake dusted with herbs and honey. The cakes hadn't scampered over to Phillip yet. She smiled at him and raised one of the menacing black glass goblets to her mouth.

Aurora hoped that humans and faeries could get along. Phillip needed to try. Maleficent might want to frighten him, but she was hardly going to poison him right in front of everyone.

Probably.

He put a spoonful of the soup into his mouth.

It was surprisingly pleasant. He took another spoonful. And another. Then he speared a few mushrooms.

By the time the honey cakes finally came, he was happy to take three.

A raven circled overhead, then swooped down to drop a rodent onto an empty plate. Prince Phillip could not help startling in horror at the mouse's open mouth and the blood matting its gray fur.

The raven landed beside the plate and began to take apart the dead mouse.

"My apologies," Maleficent said, looking down the table. "Prince Phillip, would you like some meat?"

Phillip felt a little queasy seeing the mouse's blood running over the plate and the raven's beak pulling strips of red flesh from within the fur.

"There is little enough for Diaval. He shouldn't have to share," Phillip managed to say.

"But he left you the eyes," Maleficent said. "They're the best part. A real delicacy for a raven. They pop like fish eggs in your mouth."

The table had gone quiet. The faeries stared at him eagerly, waiting.

"I prefer the heart," Phillip said.

"Phillip—" Aurora began.

But Maleficent rose from her chair. "Do you really? Diaval, you heard the man."

Diaval hopped over and dropped a small piece of flesh on Prince Phillip's plate. It was the color of a garnet and half the size of a grape.

He had made an extravagant promise to Maleficent— told her he would do whatever she asked to win her approval. He'd been willing to swear on his life that he meant Aurora no harm.

This was nothing.

He picked up the heart and put it on his tongue. Gagging once, he got it down.

"Delicacy," he said, choking a little on the word.

All along the table, faeries began to laugh. Aurora stared at him in astonishment, a smile growing on her face.

"You know how to be polite," Maleficent said finally. "I will give you that. You haven't screamed once."

Phillip didn't admit how close a thing that had been. "It's been a delightful dinner."

"I am not sure I would go so far as all that," Maleficent said.

Aurora nudged her. *"Godmother."*

She took a deep breath. "Very well. You are welcome in the Moors. Aurora may even walk you to your horse, if she'd like. But I warn you, be careful what you say. This welcome can be revoked."

Phillip supposed that was as much as he could have hoped for. He pushed back his chair and stood. "Would you walk with me?"

"With pleasure," Aurora returned.

Together, they walked away from the banquet table. A cloud of tiny faeries blew around them and away.

"You were so very good tonight," Aurora said. "And I really do think you impressed my godmother. And you ate—"

"Let's never speak of it!" he said, and she laughed.

They walked on through the night. Aurora moved through the Moors nimbly, hopping easily from stone to stone.

"I will miss you very much when you're back in Ulstead," she said.

"That's what I wanted to talk to you about. I did get a letter from home asking me to return," he said, "but I haven't replied to it yet. That's not what I came to say to you the other night."

She turned to him, frowning. "What is it, then?"

Phillip needed to say it the way he'd swallowed that mouse heart: all at once.

"I love you," he told her.

Her entire demeanor changed, shoulders tensing. "You're teasing me, aren't you? Because of everyone's fussing."

"I love you," he repeated. "I love your laugh and the way you see the best in everyone. I love that you're brave and kind and that you care more about what's true and right than what anyone thinks—"

"Stop, please," she said, shaking her head. "Your kiss didn't end the curse. It wasn't True Love's Kiss. That means you can't love me. You can't!"

"We met *once* before that," Phillip said. "And your aunts were shouting at me to kiss you. That can't possibly count."

If anything, that made Aurora look more stricken. "It's not fair! All the things I said in front of you—the way I acted. Sitting up alone at night and playing games before the fire in our underclothes! I would never have behaved that way if I thought—"

Phillip felt cold all over, cold that extended all the way from his heart to his fingertips. He had thought it was possible that Aurora wouldn't return his feelings, but he hadn't expected her to be *horrified* by his confession.

"I see," he said stiffly, and made a formal bow. "I should not have spoken. I will take my leave of you."

"Yes," Aurora agreed. "You should go."

And numbly, trying to show nothing of what he felt on his face, he did.

19

The day of the festival dawned early. Aurora awoke, kicking off her blankets. She flung open her windows, letting in a rush of sweet air that carried the scents of blooming flowers and baking bread.

None of it made her feel any better.

Every time she thought of Phillip, she had a curious sensation in her chest, as though she were wearing a too-tight corset. And it seemed she couldn't put thoughts of him aside.

The night before, she'd found herself gazing down at the fountain at the edge of the royal gardens, hoping that she would see Phillip waiting for her there. If he had been, she would have gone down and tried to explain—although she wasn't sure exactly what she would have said.

Marjory came in, smiling. "Are you eager for the festival to begin?"

"Yes," Aurora said, trying to focus on that. "Today the humans and the faeries will dance together and eat together. Surely they will see that we're not so different."

Aurora thought of what Nanny Stoat had told her: *We want enough food in our bellies to be strong, enough warmth in the winter to be hale, and enough leisure to have joy.*

But the thought of food and leisure and joy made her mind wander to the monstrous banquet of the night before. Phillip had been such a good guest that everyone had liked him. And she'd been so happy.

Until the end.

Being in love had nearly destroyed Maleficent. Denying love had destroyed King Stefan. And King Stefan's inability to love Queen Leila had probably ruined her life, too.

Love was terrifying in its power.

Love was just plain terrifying.

Marjory smiled at her, looking a little skeptical. "I hope so, Your Majesty."

For a moment, Aurora couldn't recall what they'd

been talking about. Then she remembered. Humans and faeries, getting along.

"They will," she insisted. "They must." She had to get something right.

For now, Aurora insisted on wearing a simple dress of gray wool that buttoned all the way from her neck to the floor, with pocket slits that showed the red lining.

"I will come back and put on my prettiest gown for the festival, but there's so much still to do," Aurora said, pulling it on.

"My lady, no one expects you to get dirty," Marjory replied.

"But I mean to help out any way I can," Aurora said, "and there's no telling what that might entail. I promise to return."

"See that you do," Marjory chided. "Wouldn't you be a shock to your people, dressed as you are."

Moments later, Aurora was down the stairs and in the kitchens. Despite her head cook's assurances that she wasn't needed, she helped take pies out of the oven, climbed a ladder outside to stir enormous vats of soup, and even turned a spit to help cook a mess of fresh-caught fish. Feeding the whole village was an undertaking, and the kitchens were a buzzing hive of activity.

After a breakfast of a bowl of cream, which she shared

with a castle cat, Aurora hastened out to the gardens, where servants were setting up long tables and benches for the hundreds of people expected to come. Soldiers were setting up stations to make sure no one brought weapons onto festival grounds. Ribbons and garlands of flowers were being strung from the trees.

Knotgrass, Flittle, and Thistlewit flew around, enchanting ever more ribbons and blooms. An abundance of flowers sprouted from the tops of poles. Ribbons wrapped themselves all the way around the supports of tents and the backs of chairs and occasionally the hilt of a guard's sword, to his surprise and consternation.

"Isn't it glorious?" asked Knotgrass. With a wave of her hand, more peonies rained down around a maypole, carpeting the grass in pink. "I do hope everyone behaves themselves."

Aurora hoped so, too, although she saw Thistlewit turn several bouquets of peonies into daisies. Flittle, for her part, was sneaking off to add bluebells everywhere she could, but at least she wasn't changing either of her sisters' flowers. It did seem to Aurora that there were *a lot* of flowers and *a lot* of ribbons—and more all the time. The maypole was starting to look a little bit top-heavy, and the tents were sagging under the weight of the many flowers tied to their supports.

"Aunties," Aurora said, "perhaps you've done enough decorating."

The three pixies buzzed around, frowning. "Oh, no, my dear. There's so much still to be done," said Flittle.

"Though it does take a lot of our magic," Knotgrass said. "Not that we begrudge it to you."

"Oh, no," said Thistlewit. "We would work our fingers to the bone to be the least help."

"As we always have," Flittle put in, not to be outdone. "The sacrifices that we've made—"

"I have an idea," Aurora said, interrupting them before they got too far along with their protestations of abnegation. "The riddle contest will be the first event of the festival. Perhaps you three can be in charge of that."

"Yes, of course!" Thistlewit said, drawing herself up with great self-importance. "It's our pleasure to be helpful."

Aurora watched them fly off with a heavy heart.

She'd once hoped Phillip would win the riddle contest—in fact, she'd chosen riddles as the sport because of him. But now her thoughts were tangled. She didn't know what she wanted.

Marjory waved to get her attention, drawing her from her thoughts. Aurora was surprised to see her marching across the lawns of the castle. "The kitchen staff said that I would find you here," the girl said sternly, putting her hands on her hips. "You must hasten! The first guests will be here soon, and you're still in that old thing."

Aurora glanced at the sun, which had dipped lower in the sky than she'd thought. Musicians and jugglers were setting up on the grass. Her stomach growled from a lack of food, and she recalled that she hadn't eaten since breakfast.

"Very well," Aurora said. "I'm hastening."

In her rooms, her dress was spread out on her coverlet, along with smallclothes and dressings for her hair.

Marjory insisted that Aurora take a bath and be perfumed before being laced into a gown of deep blue with a tight bodice, puffed sleeves that narrowed at her upper arms and ran to her wrists, and a low neckline that revealed her finely woven white chemise. Down her arms ran embroidery of leaf-covered vines blooming with white and pink flowers. When she moved, her full skirt swirled around her.

As Aurora drank a cup of tea and ate a slice of bread with cheese, Marjory braided her hair loosely down her back with blue ribbon, then tucked sprays of white flowers into it.

"You look like you stepped out of a story," said Marjory, pinching Aurora's cheeks to bring up the color in them.

"Now *you* sit down," Aurora said, rising, "and let me tie ribbons in *your* hair."

Marjory blushed. "Your Majesty, that wouldn't be proper."

"Oh, it won't take a moment," Aurora said, "and we have so many that would go well with your dress."

Marjory allowed herself to be convinced to sit and let Aurora weave ribbons through her hair. When they were done, Marjory looked into the queen's mirror with a shy smile, turning her head back and forth.

"Do you have plans for the festival?" Aurora asked.

"My sisters are coming up from the mill," Marjory said delightedly, "and we're going to play all the games and listen to the musicians. I hear there's a wonderful storyteller that has a tale of being turned into a magical cat!"

Aurora supposed it was a good sign that the man hadn't fled the kingdom. Maybe her godmother was right, and the experience had taught him a lesson and not harmed him any.

She *hoped* that was the case, at least.

And yet it was with some trepidation about the day ahead that she lifted the golden flower-and-leaf crown that signaled her as queen of Perceforest and the Moors and placed it on her head. With one last smile at Marjory, she headed for the palace grounds.

Musicians were playing, and jugglers were tossing shining balls into the air. Guests had arrived. Courtiers walked along the grounds in groups, with pages and maids by their sides. Villagers wandered on the grass, giggling and pointing. Children ran in packs, getting their best clothes dirty. And she saw groups of faeries, too. Faeries made of moss and bark. Pixies and hobs. Foxkin and wallerbogs and hedgehog faeries. The humans gave them a wide berth, but they were there. All of them together, receiving pennies and cakes and cups of cider from palace servants.

The cooks had begun to set out the first course of entremets. These divertissements—like castles of spun sugar, and pies that released live doves into the sky, and swans that seemed to breathe real fire—caused spectators to gasp in surprise. The children, especially, many of whom had not so much as tasted sugar before and had never seen such things, were in transports of delight.

Lady Fiora walked up to Aurora, along with Lady Sybil. Lady Fiora's black hair was braided up on her head, and she wore a gown of the palest pink. Lady Sybil wore yellow with matching ribbons and a hair caul of gold net.

"You look splendid, Your Majesty," exclaimed Lady Sybil.

"As do you," said Aurora, grinning. "Both of you."

"But you're not wearing the necklace," said Lady Fiora. "The one my brother had made for you. Didn't you like it?"

"I thought the iron was *inappropriate* for today," said Aurora stiffly.

"Ah," Lady Fiora said, changing the subject with a nervous laugh. "Are you ready for the contest?"

Lady Sybil took Aurora's hand. "Oh, you must come. Everyone's so eager."

Aurora looked toward the crowd gathered around a stage and saw Knotgrass flying over them. "Are there many contestants?"

Lady Sybil giggled. "You'll see!"

As they drew Aurora closer, she spotted Lord Ortolan waiting for her by the stage. Her aunties were there, too. The crowd gave a cry when Aurora stepped up. She grinned and waved, and the shouting got louder.

Knotgrass buzzed up to her. "Oh, Aurora, your friends had so many good ideas for riddles!"

"Ah, good," she said, realizing that though she'd asked her aunties to arrange things and hoped it would keep them from burying the festival in flowers, she had no idea just *what* they'd arranged for the contest.

"My queen!" Lord Ortolan said, pitching his voice loudly so that the audience heard him. "Your subjects await the opening contest of the festival—a contest to win your hand for a single dance, the first of today!"

At that pause, Aurora jumped in, turning to the crowd.

"Thank you for coming. I hope that all of you—my dear subjects—will drink and eat and laugh together."

Another cheer went up at her words.

Flittle, Knotgrass, and Thistlewit began explaining the contest. Many villagers and courtiers and faeries alike waited in an area separated from the rest of the crowd by ribbons, having signaled their intention to vie for a dance with the queen. From young boys to elderly men with canes, to several people Aurora suspected of being ladies with their hair tucked up in hats, to Fair Folk, at least two dozen contestants were ready to answer riddles. Count Alain was among them, leaning against the stage and whispering with three young noblemen Aurora recognized from court. Robin, too, had come, probably to represent the Moors. Possibly to confound Count Alain.

"I see that Prince Phillip won't be taking part," Lord Ortolan observed to Aurora in an undertone. "I heard a rumor that—"

"Yes. He is taking his leave of us soon," she whispered back, trying not to let him see that it bothered her.

"For our first round," said Flittle, "I shall ask a riddle and each of you will come and tell me the answer. Answer incorrectly and you leave the stage. Answer right and you remain a player."

She intoned the first of the riddles:

I saw a being
Of shining beauty.
She came over the roof
And through my window.
Then west she went,
Hurrying home.
With her gone,
Night departed.

Each contestant came forward to whisper an answer to Flittle. Some she nodded at. Others she sent away. The first round eliminated a little under half the contestants.

"The answer is the *moon*," said Thistlewit triumphantly. There were murmurs in the audience—perhaps from people who'd guessed correctly, perhaps from those who were sorry to see someone they knew lose. "I shall be the one to speak the next riddle."

She did so:

Bent over as I am,
Yet I am meant for fighting.
Loosen my string and I stand up taller.
But unstring me and I serve no one.
To do your bidding, I must be cleverly tied,
And never will I work alone.

More muttering followed from the audience. Aurora supposed that they were whispering guesses to one another and hoped they would not be so loud that the contestants would overhear.

The words of this riddle stuck in her head. Perceforest had been on the brink of war with the Moors throughout most of her childhood—and though she had been well out of it, plenty of these folks had not. And before that, things had been worse.

"The answer is a *bow*, you clever dears!" Thistlewit continued.

The initial group had been cut down quite a bit. Remaining were Count Alain and one of the other nobles, a Baron Nicholas; three men from the town, who gave their names as John, Jack, and Mark; and Robin, from the Moors.

Aurora felt a strange hollowness.

"What a good idea this is," Lady Sybil said, clapping her hands together. "I know an excellent riddle. May I ask one?"

"Of course." Thistlewit smiled at the girl, then addressed the crowd. "Now that we've narrowed down our contestants, we will ask each one a riddle. They must answer it correctly in front of everyone or be eliminated. Fail and the same riddle will pass to the contestant at your left."

Robin was up first.

"Go ahead, Lady Sybil," Thistlewit said encouragingly. With a giggle, she began:

She is sharply defended
Yet dies because of her beauty
And her mysterious perfume.
She will live on in poetry,
Decorating my mantel with her grave.

"That's quite grim," Lord Ortolan said, startled.

But the crowd seemed to enjoy it, cheering for her as she said the words.

Robin bowed with a flourish as he stepped forward to answer. "We faeries love a good riddle. And we particularly love one as pretty as this. The answer is a rose." He waved his hand in the air, calling forth three roses. They were light blue and larger than any Aurora had seen away from the Moors, including the ones Maleficent had caused to grow at the borders.

The crowd cheered as he gave one to Thistlewit, one to Aurora, and the last to the blushing Lady Sybil.

Count Alain was the next contestant to be tested as Robin walked to one side of the stage.

Lady Fiora touched Thistlewit's shoulder. "May I ask one next?"

"Indeed, dearie," said the pixie.

Aurora felt curiously listless. And she kept scanning the crowd without being quite sure what she was looking for. It was only when Lady Fiora began speaking that Aurora realized that it was probably unfair that her riddle was for her own brother.

> *A weaver with a deadly cloth*
> *She will never wear.*
> *Her larder is a living feast*
> *Of the mute victims of her art.*
> *She is blessed with eyes and hands*
> *But cursed to live always inside armor.*

Count Alain seemed to think for only a moment before he gave his answer. "A spider."

Aurora gave Lady Fiora a sidelong glance, but the girl didn't seem to notice. And what did it matter who Aurora stood up with first? If it was Alain, then so be it. If it made the other nobles think he had more influence with her or he was more in her favor, they would soon learn otherwise.

It's just a game, Aurora reminded herself. *A silly game.*

But as Knotgrass began giving a contestant another riddle, Lady Sabine walked onto the stage, dragging Prince Phillip along behind her. Aurora's stomach lurched and her heart raced.

"What is he doing here?" Lord Ortolan whispered to her.

Aurora shook her head at him and turned to listen to Knotgrass.

I am a trickster who conceals the truth
To the delight of the young and old.
I am the father of puzzles and the daughter of poems.
Solve me by speaking the name of what confounds you.

Baron Nicholas, whose turn it was, stared at Knotgrass in confusion. As the seconds passed, the crowd began to jeer. The skin of his neck got red and he looked mulish. Then he strode angrily from the stage.

John's turn came next. He guessed a jester, but that wasn't the answer, so he got jeered at in turn. Then came Jack and Mark, neither of whom had any guesses at all.

For a moment there was silence.

Then Phillip spoke. "A riddle."

He was met with cheers even before Knotgrass confirmed that he was correct.

But Phillip didn't appear pleased that he'd given the answer. And he didn't meet Aurora's gaze. In fact, he didn't resemble his usual kind and affable self at all. He seemed like a stranger to her.

"I didn't know you were engaged in this game," Count Alain said to him, not quite quietly enough that they wouldn't be overheard.

Phillip made a nonchalant shrug. "Nor did I. But Lady Sabine insisted on my not missing it."

Lady Sabine seemed to be extremely pleased with herself. No doubt she thought she had done her queen a good turn.

Aurora wasn't sure what to feel. There was a part of her that wanted to run from the stage, go off by herself, and weep, but she wasn't sure what she had to be sad about.

Who cried because a handsome prince she cared about told her that he loved her?

But she'd been afraid. And she'd hurt him because she was afraid.

And now her best friend was angry with her and it was entirely her fault.

At three contestants, the elimination process slowed down. Riddle after riddle was asked and answered.

On and on they went. Round after round.

I was before the world began
And will remain when it is gone.
You may make much of me
Or squander me,
But you will not call me back
Once I am lost.

Time.

What force and strength cannot get through,
I with a gentle touch can do;
And many in the streets would stand
Were I not, as friend, at hand.

A key.

I am a nimble creature
Who skips from tree to tree.
My tail is my glory.
Like the ant, I store for winter
In the knot of my treasury.

A squirrel.

Robin dropped out first, with a grin at Aurora that suggested he knew the answer but was going to cede the field to Phillip. She suspected he'd only entered the contest to keep Count Alain from dancing with her. Shooting an arrow into the Moors had really turned the faeries against him.

"This could be the final riddle," Flittle said, to the cheers of the audience. They'd enjoying watching the game thus far, and now that they had the promise of seeing at least one more of the nobility made a fool of, their enjoyment kicked up a notch.

"I have one," Lady Fiora said.

"No," Aurora told her firmly. "Since it's the final riddle, I ought to be the one to ask it."

Lady Fiora and Count Alain exchanged glances. Aurora took a steadying breath. She didn't like the idea of opening the dancing with Count Alain, since he could not be relied upon to be welcoming to the faeries.

Yet dancing with him would certainly be less fraught than dancing with Prince Phillip.

But Phillip had been dragged onstage by Lady Sabine; it wasn't like he was demanding anything of Aurora after his confession. And he was her friend. Maybe if she signaled to him that they were still friends, she could apologize for how she'd behaved after the banquet and they could forget about everything that had been said. Friendship was safe. If they could get back to that, they would be safe again, too.

"The answer I give is no, but it means yes. Now what is the question?" Aurora asked Prince Phillip.

He looked her directly in the eye.

"I do not know, Your Majesty," he said.

The crowd was shouting and Count Alain was eagerly answering, but all the noise seemed to come from very far away. She couldn't focus on any of it. All she could see was Phillip turning away from her and walking off the stage.

20

Maleficent arrived with her company of faeries as the sun began to dip toward evening. She wore a formidable gown of black velvet and silk, with tattered edges on her wide skirts. Diaval was on her arm, in black velvet and silver. A cuff hung from his ear, swinging back and forth in time with his gait.

Just walking onto the castle grounds gave her a deep sense of unease. The place absolutely stank of iron—so much so that even after Aurora's efforts at removing it, she couldn't help noticing the scent with a shudder. It brought back the sense memory of her skin blistering, of her helplessness when bound in its chains. It brought back the pain of her missing wings. It brought back the brutal satisfaction of standing in front of the first human she'd ever loved and finally finding a way to hurt him as badly as he had hurt her. And it brought back her standing over Aurora's sleeping body and knowing that the person she loved best might never wake.

Maleficent tried to shake off all of that. Aurora had created the festival to unite her kingdoms, and Maleficent was determined to frighten as few humans as possible.

And she had to admit the festival itself was quite charming.

Humans were everywhere, both those dressed in finery and those in homespun. The tables outside the castle were full. There were tureens of soups and elderberry jam–filled pastries in the shapes of angels and goblins, moons and towers, wolves and mermaids. There were cakes dusted with gold flakes and dotted with edible flowers. There were jellies and crèmes in jewel colors, molded into improbably tall and slightly wobbly shapes. There were fruits made of marzipan and rolled in sugar so that they shone in the candlelight.

And there was a riot of flowers everywhere — *familiar* flowers. Maleficent scowled. They were the work of Flittle, Thistlewit, and Knotgrass, she was certain. They adored their own wing colors so much they matched not only their clothing to them, but absolutely everything else. She could even see where they'd been fighting with one another: some daisies became peonies halfway across a single bloom.

A wicked smile turned up the corners of her mouth. It would be a small thing to unify the decorations. She flicked her fingers in the air, sending out sparks of magic.

All around her, the flowers began to change. The petals grew larger and darker until enormous black roses crawled over every surface that had previously been decorated with peonies, daisies, or bluebells.

"Much better," Maleficent said with satisfaction.

"Oh, yes," said Diaval. "Not menacing at all."

Faeries had begun to explore the feast. She saw some wallerbogs tasting the soup and a foxkin nibbling on the bread. One tiny winged butterfly faerie took an enormous bite out of a marzipan plum and spat it out in disgust when he realized it was made of almond paste. A tree woman was causing golden pears to bloom on her arms and offering them to passersby.

The humans appeared nervous, but not entirely ungracious. However, that nervousness turned to outright fear in Maleficent's presence. People hastened to clear a path at her approach.

Then she heard a familiar voice.

"A witch she was," he said. "And in a wave of her hand, I was no longer myself. I was a cat! That's right, the very sort that hunts for mice or sleeps by your hearth. I opened my mouth to protest, to cry out for help, but the only sound that came out was a *meowwwwwww*."

Nervous laughter followed. A few small children clapped their hands, clearly delighted at the prospect of becoming cats.

It was the storyteller Maleficent had enchanted. She walked to the edge of his crowd, raising a single eyebrow at him. This time she wore no cloak. He could see her quite clearly.

"And that began m-my adventure," he stammered, his face paling at the sight of Maleficent. He went on with the tale, obviously rattled. "I ran into the bushes. The witch hunted for me but could not discover my hiding place. Long I waited, tail twitching, trying to get used to a body that moved on all fours and was overwhelmed with smells. Luckily, cats from the neighborhood found me. I fell in with a grizzled old tom who gave me good advice. He showed me how to hunt. Soon I was happy lying in the sun, eating what I caught, drinking from streams. I even found a cat to take to wife, and we were soon expecting our first litter of kittens. My old life seemed far behind me, though I never quite got used to the fleas.

"But then this good lady, Maleficent the faerie, came upon me and turned me back into myself. And here she is, the hero of the hour. My lady, you have my thanks! Truly, this story is a tribute to you."

Maleficent was impressed and amused by the tale he'd spun out of perhaps a week spent sulking around the Moors in feline form. She bowed to both him and the crowd.

After some wandering across the grass, Diaval had acquired a mug of some foaming beverage that he was effusive in praising, and Maleficent had spotted where the dancing was to take place.

Better-dressed people milled close to a large bonfire, where a band had struck up a tune. As Maleficent approached, she saw that the nobles were even more afraid of her than the villagers had been, shrinking back, ladies in gowns clutching one another's hands. She tried to smile, but at the sight of her fangs, a woman tripped and fell into the balloon of her own dress. It took two footmen to get her up again.

Diaval had to be turned into a raven for a full five minutes to hide his laughter.

Across the way, Flittle, Thistlewit, and Knotgrass buzzed around without causing much alarm, but when a faerie piper offered his services to the musicians, she could tell that they were afraid he would lead the crowd in an enchanted dance.

And so what if he did? Maleficent thought with resentment. It might be a little uncomfortable, but at least it would get everyone on their feet.

Perhaps it would even prove that magic could be employed entertainingly.

As Maleficent considered that, the crowd began to stir. Then it parted as footmen rolled out a carpet. And behind the carpet walked Aurora in a gown of blue, her crown glinting in the torchlight. She looked regal, Maleficent thought. She looked like her mother. She even had her eyes—eyes that met Maleficent's as she stepped into the dancing area. The girl gave her a quick grin, the impish one she'd had since she was a child.

The musicians, including the faerie piper, took up a pavane.

And Count Alain stepped out to take Aurora's hand. He was dressed all in black velvet, making the stripe of white in his hair stand out. On his chest, he wore a large iron pin studded with garnets. Maleficent narrowed her eyes, recalling dangling him over the forest floor. She was sorry not to have an excuse to do it again.

Together, they began the stately steps of the dance, looking for all the world as though they were a couple.

How had he managed it? Maleficent turned her gaze to Lord Ortolan suspiciously. And indeed, he did look pleased. But she was surprised to see that behind him, Flittle, Thistlewit, and Knotgrass looked equally happy. Flittle was clasping her hands together and whispering to Knotgrass.

Stupid meddling pixies. What do they think they're doing?

In front of the crowd, Aurora and Count Alain stood side by side with their hands clasped. They bent their knees slightly toward the audience and then toward each other, heads high. Together, they took a few steps, went up on their toes, took a few more steps, and went up on their toes again. Then, parting hands, they each took a turn about the grass; then they came back and clasped hands again, spinning around each other. When Aurora stumbled, Count Alain caught her ably.

Maleficent's gaze swept the crowd. She spotted Phillip in a tunic of deep blue velvet, leaning against a flower-covered support, his gaze on Aurora unmistakably that of a boy suffering in love.

She crossed the lawn to stand beside him.

"Come to gloat?" he asked her sulkily.

"I may not like you," she said, "but I am not fool enough to prefer *him*."

Phillip gave a hollow laugh. Up close, he seemed a bit haggard. Although he was dressed in his typical princely finery, he didn't appear to have slept since the last time Maleficent saw him, at the banquet.

She narrowed her eyes. "What's wrong with you, princeling?"

"I told her," he said, "and it went just as you told me it would. I was a fool."

"What excellent news," Maleficent said. "This party grows better and better."

"At least one of us can be happy," he said. "I do not know that I will ever be happy again."

Maleficent turned to watch the dance with raised brows. As Aurora and Count Alain went through the synchronized hops and steps, she could see that the hushed crowd thought the ridiculous skunk must have Aurora's favor.

Finally, the music ended and both partners bowed slightly. Then the musicians struck up another piece—a lively galliard. The grass filled with courtly dancers. The townsfolk watched, waiting for their turn at one of the country dances.

Although there were unpartnered ladies in attendance and Prince Phillip ought to have led one of them onto the floor, he did not. Looking lovesick, he departed.

Count Alain took Aurora's hand, pulling her to him and whispering something in her ear. Even though she wasn't close, Maleficent noticed the girl's expression change to alarm. Without a glance at anyone else, Aurora allowed Alain to draw her away from the clearing and back to the palace.

Maleficent liked that even less than the dance.

"Diaval," she hissed, "we are going to follow Aurora."

"Are we, mistress? How very different from my usual orders."

She scowled at him, and he gave her a grin. It was useless trying to intimidate the raven-man these days. He knew her entirely too well.

Together, they moved through the crowd, toward the palace. Sometimes Maleficent thought she saw a flash of the girl's golden hair or her crown, but it was hard to be sure. Entering the hall from outside, she was surprised to find Prince Phillip already there, a half step ahead of her, and heading for the stairs.

"Looking for someone?" Maleficent asked, raising a single elegant brow.

He flushed. "I saw her leave with the count. She seemed upset. And I don't trust Alain."

"I will tell Aurora of your concern for her well-being when I find her," Maleficent informed him, moving past.

"I'll tell her myself," he returned. "I know the castle better than you do. You're not going to find her without me."

"I have watched over her since she was a child," Maleficent reminded him.

"You cursed her!" he snapped.

Maleficent lifted her hand, pointing a finger at him. Her nostrils flared. "And I am about to curse you!"

Prince Phillip took a deep breath. "Let me come with you," he said quietly. "Please. The last time I saw her, I upset her, and I just want things to be right between us again."

Maleficent softened. "Very well. Come. But only because I do not want to spend more time in pointless argument." With those words, she began to climb the stairs, leaving Diaval to follow her, and Prince Phillip to trail behind.

I don't trust Alain, he'd said. Maleficent didn't, either, but now she was beginning to have more specific fears. What if the count intended to abduct Aurora?

At the top of the stairs was a single tiny white flower, the kind that had been braided into the girl's hair. For a moment, Maleficent held it cupped in her palm.

"Count Alain's rooms are nearby," Phillip said. "The third door on the left. But I can't think why she would come here with him."

Maleficent thought of the spindle Aurora had once pricked her finger on. She thought of all the dangers that could not be anticipated.

She swept down the hall, Prince Phillip and Diaval on her heels.

At the door, she did not bother to check if it was locked but magicked it open in a swirl of golden sparkles. Inside the room were soldiers, ten of them at least, heavily armed. They rushed toward her.

But before she could react, an iron net fell over her from the ceiling. Pain raced through her, along with a terrible helplessness. She screamed in horror, but also with the memory of another iron net—one she knew had been destroyed.

Diaval was pulling on the net, attempting to lift it off her.

She tried to turn even as the iron scorched her skin. It glowed red where it touched her.

"Phillip, run!" Maleficent called to him. He had to get away. He had to find Aurora.

But more men-at-arms were coming up the stairs, blocking his way. She recognized one of them from the hunt. Count Alain's man.

Phillip's gaze met hers. She could see in his face that he knew just how much trouble they were in. He grabbed for a sword mounted on the wall. *You're a fool,* she thought, *but a brave fool.*

Reaching her hand through the net, she caught hold of Diaval's arm. There was only one thing she could think to do, and she hoped she had the magic for it. *"Into a raven,"* she said with a swirl of glittering gold from her fingers. "Watch over her. Warn her!"

A moment later, Diaval was gone and in his place was a black bird, his feathers gleaming. Maleficent felt queasy with exhaustion, but she'd managed it. She'd changed him. Diaval the raven cawed and flew from the landing, past soldiers who tried to grab or swung at him.

In horror, Maleficent watched as one of the blades caught the edge of his body and knocked him from the air.

Rough hands grabbed hold of his flapping wings.

A clang of metal brought her thoughts back to where

she stood. Three soldiers were trading blows with Prince Phillip. Back and forth they sallied along the narrow hall. She tried to struggle free of the net with renewed fear.

But then someone clasped her from behind and brought a rag to her face. There was a horrible sweet scent on it, the same smell that had wafted off the drink Stefan gave her on the single worst night of her life. She felt lightheaded with panic. She threw her head back, knocking her horns against the soldier behind her. They both crashed to the floor.

She crawled away from him, dragging the net with her. More arms grabbed her from behind, pushing her to the ground. The heady smell of poison intensified, and along with it came a vast dizziness.

She felt herself slipping. She looked up at Phillip just in time to see a soldier's blade pierce his side.

21

For most of his life, Diaval had been a raven. He'd lived in a community of perhaps several hundred on the outskirts of the Moors, roosting in trees, hunting for food, and jousting in the air to show his daring.

He'd been a good thief. He had stolen fruit from the orchards of humans, earthworms from the beaks of his brothers and sisters, and carrion from wolves. He remembered the thrill of it.

And he remembered the terror of being turned into a man. A farmer had been about to kill him. The transformation had saved his life, but he no longer felt as though his life was his own. Not only did he owe an impossible-to-repay debt to the faerie standing before him with the curving horns and cold eyes, but his whole self was changed.

He hated being human, but once he was, he knew emotions he hadn't known before—regret and contempt, jealousy and empathy. And he had words, which changed how he saw everything, including himself.

Then she turned him into a horse, which was distasteful, but he couldn't forget the power of that body. That changed him, too. His mind had been simpler than that of a raven, more driven by instinct. And his instinct had been to protect his mistress.

Then she turned him into a dragon, which was powerful beyond all things. It woke an ancient hunger in him and a rage big enough to devour the world—and half the beings in it. Ever after, even when he was a raven again, he couldn't forget that feeling. He felt bigger than his skin.

But what changed Diaval most of all was being by Maleficent's side. He'd learned to care for her and Aurora, whom he'd adored since she was a fledgling floundering around outside her nest. Though he'd begun his service in awe, he now stayed by Maleficent's side because there was nowhere else he would rather be.

He thought of all that as he felt a wagon lurch around him. He'd been thrown into a burlap sack, as though he were some game bird caught during a hunt.

His beak was sharp enough to wear through the cloth, so he started on that, rubbing it against the ground. It was slow work, but there was nothing else for it. He dared not move his wings to make sure they were unhurt, for fear one of the soldiers would see. He had to be patient.

Eventually, he wore a small tear in the fabric. Worming his beak through, he opened his mouth and tore the hole wider. Finally, he was able to get his head out. Then, with some ripping and wriggling, he was free. Diaval found himself in a covered cart with a back that was entirely open. Several soldiers sat on either side, their weapons pointed at two bodies on the floor. Bags were over both their heads, and Maleficent was wrapped in heavy chains.

He wanted to save her, but what could he do? If he tried to peck out their eyes, they would likely recapture him or kill him. And he couldn't manage to blind more than two.

I expect you not to fail me.

Well, he didn't intend to. He would go and find Aurora, and together they would save Maleficent.

With that in mind, he sprang up from the floor of the cart and hoped his wings weren't damaged, hoped they could carry him into the air. And when they did, he gloried in the shouts of the soldiers below. They would see him again—and hopefully when they did, Maleficent would turn him into a dragon and they would know what it was like to run from his fire.

Flying back toward the castle, he thought of what it would be to lose her. He recalled his last sight of Maleficent, caught in the iron web of netting, her horns pulling against it, her eyes wide and bright with fury.

He would save her. He must save her.

For the first time, he would have traded away his ravenness forever to be a man who could speak. Who could fight. Who could do something more than circle in the sky, searching for the gleam of a gold crown and hoping that somehow Aurora would be able to understand him.

22

Aurora hurried after Count Alain as he led her toward the palace, changing directions abruptly halfway there. When he'd told her that one of his people had overheard Simon's family arguing with a group of faeries, she'd followed him without question.

"You ought to have told me before the dancing began," Aurora said. "Who knows what's happened without us intervening!"

He accepted her criticism without comment. And then there was nothing to say, because she saw two groups shouting at each other. Humans stood face to face with Fair Folk, both groups appearing to be frothingly angry.

"All we want is our child back!" Simon's father yelled into the face of a tree warrior. The faerie's features were seemingly carved out of bark, with moss hanging off the side of his head like oddly cut hair.

"We've told you a score of times, we don't have your pup," piped up a mushroom faerie.

"We'd prefer not to fight," Simon's father said, "but we will if we must. We know about your weakness when cut with cold iron."

There came a hiss from the nearby faeries at this threat.

"We know about your weakness when enchanted," said a pixie with green wings and sharp teeth.

Never had Aurora been so glad that she'd had the foresight to forbid weapons from the festival.

"No one wants violence of any kind," said Count Alain, to Aurora's surprise. The crowd turned to see him and, noticing their queen standing to his side, bowed hastily.

"You are mistaken. The faeries do not have your boy," Aurora told Simon's family. "My own soldiers have sworn to me there's no sign that faeries took him, but rather that it was the work of brigands."

Simon's father looked surprised, but he didn't seem ready to believe her words.

"We told you!" said a hedgehog faerie, wrinkling his nose. "What do we want with a poxy human boy?"

That seemed about to set off Simon's father again when Nanny Stoat arrived. She moved to stand next to Aurora.

"You heard the queen," she said, making a shooing motion. "Time to disperse."

"But one of the soldiers told me it was them," Simon's father said. "He said that those faeries there were the ones who carried off my child."

"Who told you that?" Aurora asked.

Simon's father looked around the festival desperately but then seemed confused. "I don't know. He was here a moment ago."

"It's not true," Aurora said.

Simon's father's expression turned mulish. "But he said—"

"Is that a way to talk to your sovereign ruler?" Nanny Stoat asked him, emphasizing her point by poking him in the leg with the end of the walking stick she held.

He shook his head, looking more repentant after her reprimand than he had following anything Aurora said.

Gathering himself up, he raised his eyes to Aurora's. "You will tell me if you hear more news of him, won't you? And you won't stop looking?"

"I won't stop looking," Aurora said, although from what her castellan had told her, she wasn't sure that anything more they heard would be at all good.

After he left, she turned to Nanny Stoat. "Thank you," she said. "Without your support, I am not sure they would have believed me half as readily." She looked around. "I hope this festival wasn't foolish."

"No," Nanny Stoat told her. "We ought to be like this, all together. Even if we squabble. And it does the people good to see their queen having fun."

Aurora smiled at that. "I am not sure what my court makes of me, let alone my people."

"They think you're young and a little foolish," she replied. "And entirely too comfortable with the common folk. Not to mention the Fair Folk."

Aurora wrinkled her nose. "And I wasn't sure I wanted to know, either."

The old woman laughed.

"I don't know how to make any of them listen to me the way they listen to you," Aurora said with a sigh.

"You will," said Nanny Stoat. "But changing their minds is something else. You might see the beauty in magic, while some people will only ever see the power in it."

With that, Nanny Stoat walked off, leaning on her

walking stick for support. The crowd was still breaking up. Count Alain remained by Aurora's side.

"Thank you for bringing me here and for knowing that I'd want to come," she told him. "I didn't think you understood."

"Because of the necklace?" he asked her.

She thought of the arrow he'd shot into the Moors and the rage on his face. "For one thing."

He took her hand. "My queen, I have lived my whole life thinking of the faeries as monsters. To see them differently isn't easy for me, but you have made me want to try. I should have considered my gift to you more carefully, but as it is the metal mined in my lands, I have a special affinity for it."

"I am glad you're trying," Aurora said, smiling up at Count Alain. She recalled how she'd thought that if she could convince him to see the benefits of allying with the Fair Folk, then it would be possible to convince the rest of her kingdom. She'd given up on that after the gift of the necklace, but it seemed she'd succeeded after all. She ought to be pleased.

But it was impossible for her to feel much of anything when she still needed to make things right with Phillip.

She'd spotted him during her dance with Alain. It had

been all she could do not to rush from the dance to chase him down and explain things. She knew she shouldn't have spoken so harshly to him after the banquet in the Moors. She owed him an apology.

But first she had to find him.

When she returned to the dancing area, a branle was being performed, the participants moving back and forth in a wide circle, up onto their toes and down again. Phillip was neither among the dancers nor among those watching. Her godmother was nowhere to be seen, either, but there was some time before the signing ceremony.

With a sinking heart, Aurora danced the gavotte, the saltarello, and several caroles. Her spirits lowered with each one, although a tree man spun her with such grace that she never lost her footing. And yet, she could see that her plan was working. She wasn't the only human partnered with a faerie. Nor were all the dancers noble. For her last set, she was partnered with a sturdy farmer who clearly couldn't believe his luck and guided her through the steps with aplomb.

When it was done, she excused herself from the floor. Phillip hadn't returned. She meant to look for him in another area of the festival, but before she could, Lady Fiora brought her a cup of cider. Immediately, she began discussing the nobles who had come, and telling Aurora how beautiful she had looked on the floor.

"I shouldn't say this, but my brother stared so while you danced," Lady Fiora said with a giggle. "And you are beautifully flushed. Your eyes are positively sparkling."

"Have you seen Prince Phillip?" Aurora asked before gulping down the drink.

Lady Fiora looked surprised. "Why, I thought he'd gone," she said. "Back to Ulstead."

Aurora's heart seemed to twist.

"Did I say something—"

"Excuse me." Aurora raced away from the dancing and across the lawn, past jugglers and an impromptu wrestling match between a hedgehog faerie and a burly human who seemed surprisingly equal in both strength and agility, past the storyteller Maleficent had uncursed, who was telling a tale about a fish with a ring in its stomach. But Phillip was nowhere she looked.

It was hard for Aurora to move through the crowd without someone stopping her to tell her either how lovely the festival was and how much they were enjoying it or to make a request that she do something about, say, their neighbors' goats always grazing on their land.

But Aurora paused long enough only to smile or thank

the person or say that she couldn't help them right then. And with each step, her feeling of panic intensified.

She spotted Flittle near a large basin where children were laughing and bobbing for apples.

"Have you seen Phillip, Auntie?" she asked.

"No, my dear," said Flittle. "Is he lost?"

Aurora moved on, but at every turn there was someone to engage her in conversation.

"Did you see what Lord Donald of Summerhill is wearing?" asked Lady Sybil. "He's got on a jacket with sleeves so long they're dragging in the dirt!"

"Beauteous Queen Aurora, whose hair resembles nothing so much as the wheat of fertile fields, I was devastated to lose the riddle contest," said Baron Nicholas. "But though I could not have the first dance, perhaps I can have this one. Won't you step out with me?"

"I see the reason for the treaty now," said Balthazar the tree man. "Not before, but now."

"What a marvelous festival this is," said Thistlewit. "Come and take a piece of cake with your favorite auntie."

Prince Phillip had left Perceforest. She wouldn't ever get to say farewell to him.

She sagged down onto the grass.

All around her the festival went on, but the sounds of it seemed to recede in her ears. She could think of only one thing—*she loved Phillip.* The very thing she had feared, the very thing she'd thought she was protected from, had happened.

She had looked for him in moments of distress, sought him out when she was in need of cheering up. She had laughed with him and told him her fears and hopes. And she had loved him all the while, not knowing that was love. But now she had lost him forever, for want of the courage to know her own heart.

Above her head, a raven circled, cawing to get her attention. Diaval landed in front of her, hopping and waving his wings.

"What is it?" she asked him, moving close and bending toward him. "Has something happened?"

A few people looked at her, thinking that it was very strange to see their queen expecting answers from a bird. She waited for him to become a man, but he didn't change. He just kept hopping and dancing and squawking wildly.

A terrible dread filled her.

"Nod your head twice if Maleficent is in danger," Aurora said.

Diaval bobbed his head twice.

"Take me," Aurora said. "I'll follow."

23

The raven spun up into the air, flying off toward the stables and then circling back, as though checking to be sure Aurora was heading in the right direction. The *stables*? Did Diaval intend for her to ride? How far could Maleficent be from the castle?

"My queen," said Lord Ortolan, stepping into her path, "is something amiss?"

"Yes," she said distractedly. "My godmother."

Aurora spotted Nanny Stoat standing near one of the long tables where villagers sat to partake of the festival food. Near her was Hammond, the man caught poaching in her woods, and a girl she judged to be his daughter. The girl was about Aurora's size, dressed in homespun and heavy boots. "I must help her."

"Now?" Lord Ortolan asked, looking around in bafflement. "But this is your festival. Are you saying that the signing of the treaty must be delayed? Did something happen?"

The treaty. In her horror over the thought of Maleficent in danger, she'd almost forgotten. If they didn't sign now — that night — would it seem as though someone had broken the peace? It came to her that perhaps foiling the treaty was the *motive* for whatever had happened. That thought only deepened her dread.

"Your pardon," Aurora said to the girl in the homespun, thinking of Diaval's leading her to the stables. "Would you be willing to trade your clothes for mine?"

The girl looked up at her in confusion. "Your clothes?"

"Yes," Aurora said.

Nanny Stoat jabbed the girl in the side. "Gretchen, you ought to agree. Her dress would pay off a chunk of your family's debts."

"Yes, but I can't possibly —" The girl, Gretchen, shut her mouth and curtsied. "Of course, my queen. Yes. My clothes. And thank you for your kindness to my father."

Hammond smiled and put his hand on Gretchen's arm.

"Your Majesty, we'd be happy to give you the shirts off our backs, but surely you'd prefer your own?"

"Not today," Aurora said. "Nanny Stoat, I want you to be in charge for the length of time that I am gone."

Lord Ortolan cleared his throat. "You cannot seriously mean—"

But she cut him off before he could finish. "I do." Aurora removed the crown from her head and set it down in front of the old woman. "They'll listen to you. And they should. Tell them that the signing will happen—there's just been a delay. You won't let them forget we have much in common."

"Including some common enemies," Nanny Stoat said, glancing at the advisor.

Aurora didn't have time to dwell on that. She went into the tent and quickly exchanged clothing with Gretchen.

As they returned, Gretchen was still marveling over an embroidered silken slipper. Hammond smiled to see her dressed in such finery.

"Your Majesty," he said as Aurora was about to head for the stables, "there's something—not sure if it's important . . ."

She paused.

He reached into a sack and brought out a knife. Then he held it out to her hilt-first. "I found this."

The knife didn't appear to be very sharp or finely made. The metal was dull. She frowned at it, growing angrier by the moment. She had *explicitly* forbidden weapons. But something else about it bothered her. Iron. It was a knife forged of cold iron.

The thing was an affront. And the person who had brought it wanted to disrupt the treaty, and maybe do something far worse than that.

"He won't get in trouble, will he?" Gretchen asked, her hand on her father's arm.

"Of course not," Aurora said. "Why would he?"

"It was one of the nobles who dropped it," Hammond said. "But I knew he'd deny it if I told a guard."

"Can you describe him?" Aurora asked.

Hammond frowned. "Not his face. But he was a young man with light brown hair, dressed in blue. For a moment, I thought he noticed he'd dropped the weapon, but then he kept on walking. Like maybe he was getting rid of it."

Aurora turned the knife over in her hand, wondering if it had anything to do with Maleficent's disappearance. "I'm glad you told me."

After that, Aurora went to find Smiling John. The castellan was sitting at a long table, a mug in one hand and a portion of eel pie in the other. Soldiers had gathered around him, telling stories of campaigns. They stopped abruptly as Aurora approached.

She didn't have time to do more than pull him aside and explain the situation briefly. He didn't like the idea of her riding alone in search of her godmother, and he liked the knife even less, but he eventually agreed to her plans. At least he accepted that Nanny Stoat was in charge, and was willing to reluctantly execute the rest of Aurora's orders.

Lady Fiora was waiting for her as she walked away from the soldiers. "Everyone is looking for — *What are you doing in those clothes?*"

Aurora almost laughed. "I'm afraid I must go."

"No, wait," Lady Fiora said. "Stay. I hope this has nothing to do with Phillip. There is something amiss. My brother, he —"

"Nothing to do with Phillip," Aurora said, cutting her off. "And I really, really have to go."

Aurora led her horse out to the cobbled road in front of the castle and made ready to swing up onto her back.

"My lady," said someone with a familiar voice. It was Count Alain, leading his own horse from the stables. He had a slim sword swinging from his belt.

"What a surprise," Aurora said. She wondered if he'd

come to intervene on behalf of Lord Ortolan, although he wouldn't need a horse for that. "I just ran into your sister. You're very good to see me off."

"I understand that your godmother is gone," he said. "You believe she came to misfortune."

"Her raven is going to lead me to her," Aurora told him, "whatever has happened."

"You can't be thinking of going alone?" he asked.

She put up her chin. "I am."

"Let me come," said Count Alain. "No matter what I think of the Fair Folk, I know that no one should ever head into danger without a friend by their side."

Aurora considered his offer. She thought of all she knew about him, all she feared might have befallen her godmother, and all her godmother's warnings. But Aurora had already sent Phillip away. She didn't have it in her to send away anyone else.

"It would be a great kindness if you would accompany me," she said.

24

Maleficent woke to pain worse than the iron net had caused, worse than iron chains. Her body burned. Every breath scalded her lungs. There was a spasming tightness in her muscles, and her head pounded so loudly she had difficulty thinking past it. She was in a prison of iron: the floor, the walls, and the bars were all made of the stuff.

"Maleficent?" a voice said, familiar but unsteady. "Is that you moving?"

She realized that she would have been burned worse had someone not put a bundle of cloth under her cheek, had someone not placed her hands so that they were on her chest and not the floor.

On the other side of the cell sat Prince Phillip of Ulstead, pressed against a metal wall. He was awake, his eyes shining in the gloom. His hand was against his side, where she'd seen a blade sink into him. He must be hurt, but perhaps not as badly as she'd feared.

A horn scraped against the ground as Maleficent shifted into a sitting position. She tried to make sure the cloth of her gown was between her skin and the iron floor. Part of her wanted to stand, to declare herself ready for whatever came, but the dizziness she felt just being upright told her how unwise it would be to push herself further.

If only she had her magic . . . If she had her magic, she would make them all pay.

"Are you badly hurt?" she asked.

Phillip shook his head and then, appearing to think she might not be able to see him, said, "I don't think so. I got lucky. One of the soldiers stuck a blade through my side, but it went cleanly in and out. I wrapped it with some of my shirt, and the bleeding seems to have stopped." His tone had the calm, relentless cheerfulness she'd disliked in him, but right then, in the face of unknown dangers, it was a relief. "How about you?"

"The iron," she said, not even bothering to pretend.

Phillip's expression was sympathetic, his gaze focused past her shoulder. He couldn't see her, Maleficent realized. Human eyes weren't made for darkness.

"Do you have anything that could be a weapon?" he asked her.

"I suppose we could scrape one of your bones against the floor until it was sharp as a knife." As soon as the words were out of her mouth, she regretted them. It wasn't an unreasonable question for him to have asked. She shouldn't be threatening him just because it made her feel a little better.

Although it did make her feel a little better.

A sound came from the door—a scratching, then metal against metal, as though a key was turning in a lock. In the distance, she heard a cry, like that of a boy.

Then the door opened and light flooded the room.

Phillip flinched back, closing his eyes and throwing his arm up to shield them.

Maleficent's eyes adjusted perfectly well, so she was able to see Lord Ortolan walk into the room with two prison guards holding torches.

She bared her fangs, a hiss crawling up her throat.

Aurora's advisor had seemed harmless enough to

Maleficent: a scurrying scribe, an old man who wished to return to the glories of King Stefan as uselessly and impossibly as he might wish to return to the glories of his own youth. He had seemed a nuisance, nothing more.

How annoying to be wrong.

"Your surprise gratifies me," Lord Ortolan told her, "as so little does these days."

"Just what do you think you are doing, locking me in a cage?" Maleficent asked. "Do you hope to keep Aurora from my wicked influence? She won't thank you for it. In fact, I rather think she will make the little you have left of your life a misery—if I don't manage it first."

"Care to make a small wager?" Lord Ortolan said. "Because I'd put the odds on my having more time left to me than you or the prince."

"Just what do you mean by that?" Phillip demanded.

"With both of you conveniently removed from the palace, little Aurora will marry Count Alain. And when he's king, there will be no more ridiculousness. He will return to war with the Moors. His iron will once again be in high demand, and the world will go on as it ought."

"Iron mines," said Phillip. "That's right. Alain has that land full of iron. No wonder he doesn't want peace."

"But what do you want, counselor? What will you be given for delivering us into his hands?" Maleficent asked.

Lord Ortolan snorted. "You are mistaken. This is my plan—and he, my pawn. It might have been any of the noble families who worked hand in glove with me in the time of King Stefan and Queen Leila. What I intend is to do as I have always done and have a hand in trade and taxes and tariffs. And when my time is done, I will pass down my role to a nephew whom I have groomed for the part. Gold is always more powerful than iron."

"How dull," Maleficent told him. "And how naive. I doubt that proud Alain will want anyone around him who knows what he really did to get the throne. It is not, after all, nearly as heroic a story as murdering a monster from the Moors." She paused, contemplating. "And of course, that's all assuming that Aurora will have him."

"She was once a biddable enough girl," Lord Ortolan said, although he didn't sound certain. "And she will be again, following the tragedy ahead. Her dear prince Phillip abducted her godmother and murdered her. Terrible, no? But I've made sure the evidence will bear it out. Still, he might have convinced her of his innocence. Unfortunately, he will be slain by her royal guards before she can interrogate him.

"Once you're gone, she will stop caring so much about the Moors. She'll make a lovely wife, especially once she has children to distract her. She's nothing like you."

Maleficent gave him her most menacing smile, the one that showed off her fangs. "Oh, that's true enough. She's nothing like me. But if there's one thing I know, it's that it's very foolish for the wicked not to be afraid of the good. I, for one, find goodness very alarming. And unlike you, Sir Ortolan — or me — Aurora is very, very good."

25

Moonlight allowed Aurora and Count Alain to ride over the familiar roads outside the castle until dawn broke. Then they rode through the day, Diaval making urgent circles above them. Toward night, the raven landed on the back of Aurora's horse and rode there for a while before perching on her shoulder, his black feathers fluttering in the wind.

He led them to the west, and soon they were out of the boggy wet around the Moors and into deep pine forests. But as sunset fell over unfamiliar roads, the way became harder to pick out and exhaustion began to overtake them.

"Are we close yet?" Aurora asked Diaval. Though they'd stopped at intervals to let the horses drink and eat grass, she was sure that they had been pushed to their limit as well. "Caw once if we have much farther to go."

The raven was silent, making Aurora blink herself alert.

"We ought to make camp for the night," Count Alain said. "Whatever we must face, we need to be rested for it."

"Just a little farther," she insisted.

The moon was bright enough to light their path, Aurora thought. Their horses kept on.

"You're very determined," said Count Alain. "Many girls might not be so eager to save the murderer of their father."

"You weren't there," Aurora said. "You don't understand. She tried to save him, but he was beyond saving. He loved her once and then he hated her, but his hate was some malignant thing, fed by the love. He cut the wings off her back. Can you imagine doing that to the person you cared for?"

Count Alain looked at her with a strange expression on his face. "Ambition drives people to do many things."

"King Stefan—my father—hung the wings up in his chambers, like some horrific trophy. He spoke to them, as though he was speaking to her—or to himself—I don't know. The servants told me as much. I think betraying the person he loved most drove him mad."

Count Alain shook his head. "Faeries have great powers of enchantment."

"No. I don't believe he was enchanted," Aurora said. "I saw him torture her. He had become the monster he let people believe that she was. And yet she would not have killed him. No matter what people believe of her, I know who she really is."

Alain was quiet, leading his horse on.

"She is kind," Aurora said. "More than kind. She loved me, despite my being Stefan's daughter. I don't know what I would have become without that love."

"What do you mean?"

"Maybe I would have made the same mistakes my father made," said Aurora. "Love teaches us how to love."

Count Alain was silent again for a long moment, as though he was contemplating that. "Although, in that tale, love brought her little but grief."

Aurora frowned. "You're right. But that was his fault, not hers. How could she have known? She did nothing wrong."

Suddenly, the raven sprang from her shoulder into the sky, cawing.

The pine trees had thinned out, and a worn road cut

through the terrain. "What is it, Diaval? Are we here?"

But as she looked around, she neither saw nor heard anything unusual.

The raven cawed, landing and pecking at the earth.

Aurora swung down from her horse's back and walked to the spot where Diaval stood. The raven cawed again, scratching his claws against the soil.

"Where is she?" Aurora asked him. "I don't understand! Oh, Diaval, if you would just turn back into a man and tell me."

But that just made the raven jump around more frantically.

Count Alain let out a massive sigh. "We've followed this bird for a night and a day. I am afraid it doesn't know where its mistress is."

"He knows," Aurora said, certain. "But perhaps he can't tell us."

"Well, if he can't, then he's little use." Count Alain jumped down from his horse.

Aurora paced around the spot, then stomped with one booted foot. "Hello!" she shouted. "Is anyone there?"

Only silence greeted her call.

"Maybe there will be more to see in the morning. Let's make camp," Count Alain suggested once more. "I will get up a fire. There was a stream not too far back for the horses to drink from. And we can have a meal and rest a little."

Aurora wanted to keep going, keep looking, but she had no idea how. Perhaps Count Alain was right. Maybe things would make more sense in the morning. Things often did.

"I'll gather up some firewood," Aurora said, glad of a chance to walk after riding for so long.

It was a familiar task, one she'd done often as a child. Along the way, she found a few mushrooms. But as she filled the pockets of her borrowed dress, she thought of the foraged mushrooms she'd eaten in the Moors at the banquet with Prince Phillip.

I love you. I love your laugh and the way you see the best in everyone. I love that you're brave and kind and that you care more about what's true and right than what anyone thinks —

If only she could have said something to him before he departed . . .

When Maleficent was found, she would write to him in Ulstead. Or arrange a state visit. She would find an excuse to see him. And then she would admit that she loved him. And that she'd been afraid.

And she would hope.

The last time she had seen Phillip, he'd been speaking with her godmother. It had been during her dance with

Alain, and Aurora could have sworn she saw a smile pulling up a corner of her godmother's lips.

Aurora stopped abruptly in the woods, recalling the memory again with new significance.

Had Phillip been the last person to see her godmother? Did he know something about her disappearance? Had he been taken, too?

With unsteady steps she returned to the clearing. Count Alain had already kindled a small fire. She set down the wood she'd harvested.

Diaval wasn't by the fire or circling in the sky. Diaval wasn't anywhere.

"Have you seen the raven?" Aurora asked.

Count Alain gave a nonchalant shrug. "Went off to find some carrion, I suppose. Or worms. Or whatever they eat."

Going to the fire, she took a stick and began to thread on mushrooms. It wasn't much, but at least her stomach would have something in it. "Would you like some?" she offered.

Count Alain smiled. "We can do better than that," he said, rising. From the saddlebags of his horse, he produced a pigeon pie, a bottle of port, and a thick hunk of cheese.

"Oh!" she said. "How did you think to provision yourself so well? You can't have known you were about to go on a journey."

He appeared surprised by her question, then laughed. "Yes, well observed! No, I didn't know I would be venturing out here with you, but luckily I did think I would be riding to my own estates. As I said before, I hoped to convince you to come for a visit. I thought I might ride out and prepare my people for your potential arrival."

She frowned at that, not sure what to think. Still, she was happy to eat well. Soon the fire was crackling merrily and she was wrapped in a blanket, her stomach full.

"You were good to come with me," she told Count Alain. "Especially when I know you do not care much for my godmother."

"I like her no less than she likes me," he said.

"Do you suppose Prince Phillip could be with her?" she asked. "He was not her favorite person either, but I saw them together when we were dancing. He might have been the last person to see her before whatever befell her happened."

He frowned. "Phillip?"

"Your sister told me he went back to Ulstead, but what if he only intended to leave? If she was abducted and he was with her, he might have been taken, too."

Count Alain gave that some thought. "You may be right about Phillip. But I fear he may not be the subject of misfortune, but rather its architect."

"What do you mean?" she asked.

"Well, about a half hour after you and I parted, I saw Phillip walking toward your godmother, and there was an expression on his face I am not sure I can describe. Grim purpose, perhaps. And there was something in his hand. Some kind of dull metal. If he was the one who took Maleficent, it would explain their going missing at the same time. And it would give Ulstead power over Perceforest."

Aurora listened to him in horror, thinking of the cold iron blade that had been found. Surely that couldn't have belonged to Phillip. Surely he would never do such a wretched thing.

But wasn't that what Maleficent had once thought about Stefan? Wasn't that what was so dangerous about love: that it made you vulnerable to betrayal?

Count Alain went on. "If that's what he's done, he's probably making for the border between your lands and his. Perhaps the significance of this place is that it's where the raven lost the trail. It's possible Phillip did something to throw us off the track."

Aurora was trying to think of a reason it couldn't be true. "But Phillip . . ."

"Always seemed so kind?" Count Alain said, a slight sneer in his voice. "I have heard things about Ulstead. You may think that your people are suspicious of faeries, but there they are *despised*."

In Ulstead, the stories of faeries are even worse than those told here, and there are no Fair Folk to contradict them. He'd spoken those words. But what if he also believed those tales?

Aurora recalled the night she had discovered Phillip in the Moors.

I had to see you, he'd told her. But what if he'd gone there not expecting to find her at all? What if he'd gone for a more sinister reason?

What if he'd spent the entire banquet thinking about how he hated the faeries he was dining with?

What if Aurora's rejection of him was the final straw? Reluctantly, she thought of Lord Ortolan's warning.

You may have noticed that Prince Phillip has been dangling after you. I believe he is here to win your land for Ulstead through marriage. Be wary of him.

"I can see I've upset you," said Count Alain.

Aurora picked at the cheese and did not answer.

"We are not so far from my estate," said Count Alain. "Let's make for it in the morning. I will put my soldiers at your disposal. If Phillip has Maleficent, we'll recover her. And if you must make war on Ulstead, your country will be behind you."

Aurora thought of the moment when she'd discovered

Maleficent's wings trapped in King Stefan's chamber, beating against their cage as though they were living things, independent of Maleficent. She had felt such immense horror, looking at them.

Before that, Aurora had never understood what great evil truly was. But it looked like chains of cold iron. It looked like King Stefan, hurling Maleficent across the room, intent only on causing her more pain. It looked like a desire to destroy that was greater even than a desire for power or pride.

She tried to picture that expression on Phillip's face and shuddered. Aurora was the one who had asked Maleficent to trust humans again. If only Maleficent hadn't loved Aurora, she would be safe now.

Maybe true love was a weapon after all, no matter whom you loved.

"I will save my godmother," she swore to Count Alain. "No matter who I have to face."

"I know you will," he said, taking her hand and gazing deeply into her eyes.

26

When Lady Fiora had been a little girl, her older brother, Alain, had been her whole world. Their mother had been of a nervous disposition and found an energetic child tiring in all but the smallest of doses. Their father had barely ever been home, busy at the palace in the service of King Henry and then King Stefan. And Fiora's nurse and tutor had been frequently exasperated with her wildness and inattention. Alain had been the one who taught her how to ride, the one who played games with her, teased her, and made her laugh. In return, she'd worshipped him.

After the death of their parents, she'd begged and begged until he finally brought her to court. There she tried to advance his interests. It wasn't difficult. Most nobles already admired him, which seemed exactly right. To Lady Fiora, it was Alain's due that everyone should adore him the way she did. When he'd declared his intention to win the hand of a queen, that had seemed right, too. Of course he would make the best possible king of Perceforest. Of course Aurora would love him.

So when Alain asked Fiora to do certain things, she didn't mind. Dropping a word about Prince Phillip in Aurora's ear during the ride through the woods, for example. Or apologizing for her brother. Or encouraging Aurora to choose Alain for her first dance. She was only helping both of them realize they would be perfect together.

And hoping to cheer her brother up. Because despite having brought her to court and occasionally asking her to intercede for him with other nobles, he ignored her a great deal of the time. He'd grown irritable. He would shut himself up with hoary Lord Ortolan for hours on end, becoming quite short with her if he was interrupted. And when he wasn't with Lord Ortolan, he seemed to prefer to be alone. She'd spotted him heading out on errands late at night, and when she inquired where he was going, his answers were guarded.

Perhaps he's desperately in love with Aurora, she thought, and redoubled her efforts to push them together.

But at the festival, his mood went from bad to worse. Alain had demanded she tell Aurora that Prince Phillip had left for Ulstead. He'd gripped her hard around the wrist and looked into her eyes in a way that frightened her. But it had obviously been important, so she'd done it.

The moment the words were past her lips and she saw Aurora's expression, she regretted saying them. *Well,* she reasoned, trying to convince herself she'd done the right thing, *Aurora liked him. They were close. It must be painful to find out he left, but someone had to tell her. And now the way is clear to love my brother.*

And yet, as Aurora walked off, Fiora couldn't help remembering the way that Alain's fingers dug into her skin and the desperation in his eyes. Just thinking about it made her uncomfortable.

Heart beating fast, Lady Fiora went into the palace and up the winding stairs to Prince Phillip's rooms. *I just want to see for myself that he's gone,* she thought, refusing to closely consider why she doubted it.

And, truly, she expected his rooms to be empty. But when a servant opened Prince Phillip's door, she peered inside. To her horror, she saw his trunks still resting in one corner. Books were piled up on his desk, beside a half-finished note. A sword was propped against a dresser. If Phillip was gone, why had he left all his things behind?

Fiora tried to come up with some explanation. She knew she ought to say something to Aurora, but what? She couldn't speak against her beloved brother.

She just couldn't.

And she tried to stop Aurora from leaving. But when that didn't work, and Alain rode out with her, Fiora's guilt grew worse.

Everything had gone wrong, and she didn't know how to fix it.

That night, Lady Fiora used her key to let herself into her brother's rooms. His doorframe was marked with a fresh cut in the wood. She ran her fingers over it. Just inside, she spotted a smear of blood at the corner of a carpet.

She knew he hadn't been hurt, because she'd seen him before he left. But if he wasn't the one who'd been wounded . . .

Horrified, she went to his desk, hoping to find answers. Atop it was a silver jardiniere bearing the royal crest, filled with nib pens and blocks of sealing wax. But only the most mundane and dull correspondence was within. His armoire and bedside table were equally orderly. She had turned to go when she noticed that one of the paintings near Count Alain's bed was askew.

Fiora walked over to straighten it when a thought struck her.

She took the painting down from the wall. Resting it on the bed, she turned it over.

And there, bound to the back of the frame, was a stack of correspondence from Lord Ortolan.

When she took up the first of the letters, her breath caught.

If it weren't for Stefan's purporting to have slain Maleficent, your father would have been named King Henry's heir, it read. *Remember that when you kill her. And if the boy follows, make sure you kill him, too.*

27

That night, lying by the fire and wrapped in her waxed cloak, Aurora listened to the crackle of the kindling and turned on the hard ground. With her godmother missing and Phillip implicated in her disappearance, it seemed more impossible than ever that she would sleep. But she had been awake for far too long, and her body knew it. Her eyes drooped closed.

Aurora dreamed she was wandering through the woods. Dawn was turning the horizon gold, and a light frost covered the green plants.

On she walked, her steps crunching frozen leaves. She

came to the place where Diaval had stopped the night before. But now the area was covered in ravens.

Closer she crept. The stillness of the forest made her try to be quiet, too.

Dozens and dozens of ravens cawed at her approach. And beneath their shining black feathers, she saw a pale hand sticking out of the freshly turned earth.

Aurora rushed forward. "Godmother!" she cried.

The ravens took to wing at once, in a great rush. Aurora fell onto her hands and knees. A body had been shallowly buried in the soil. Frantically, she brushed dirt away from it.

But it wasn't her godmother she found.

Prince Phillip lay stiffly, not sprawling as one does in natural rest. His face was turned upward and cold to the touch. His skin was the bluish white of skimmed milk, especially around his eyes and mouth. His chestnut curls still shone, even with dirt in them. Sunlight caught in his lashes, turning them to gold. Yet he remained as still as the grave.

"Wake up," she said in a whisper. And then, in a shout: "Wake up!"

At her shout, the ravens began to caw from the trees above.

"Be silent," she yelled at them.

And she knew that this was no enchanted sleep. This was death.

She leaned down. Some of her hair fell over his cheek and throat. Were he alive, it might have tickled him.

Taking a quick breath, she brushed her mouth against his cold, soft lips.

Then, sitting up, she prepared herself to take one last look at him. But when she gazed down, he no longer had the same appearance as before. His lips were no longer bluish, but the pink of the inside of a shell. And as she watched, his skin took on a flush of warmth.

Then, impossibly, Phillip's eyes opened, and he sucked in an unsteady breath.

"Aurora," he said, grabbing her shoulder hard enough that it hurt, "run. He's right behind you. *Run!*"

28

No torch burned in the prison. No oil lamp flickered. No window showed the stars. Phillip wasn't even sure it was night anymore. It was hard to calculate anything in complete darkness. Instead, he sat against the cold metal wall and tried to think.

His side still pained him, but it was a dull pain now, not like the burn of the wound during the ride, when his head had been covered and his hands bound. Then he'd known he was still bleeding and hadn't been sure how much, only that he could feel the wetness in the way his

shirt stuck to him. He'd been passing into and out of con-
sciousness, mostly from shock. And then there had been
the brief moment when the bag was pulled off his head in
the prison and he'd seen the horror of Maleficent sprawled
on the iron floor, her skin burning like she was a piece of
meat thrown onto a hot pan.

A moment later, the torches were doused and he was
plunged into endless night. He'd bitten at the ropes around
his hands until he was free, and then crawled across the
floor to Maleficent. He'd shucked off his doublet and pillowed her head on it, using a strip of the lining to bind
his own wound. He'd counted to ten and twenty and one
hundred, to try to calm his racing heart and focus.

Now that Maleficent was awake, he felt a little calmer.
Still, they were in fresh trouble. Phillip had feared they
would be killed as soon as they were taken, but something
had stayed the hands of their captors. Now he suspected it
was only that Lord Ortolan was waiting for Count Alain.
Perhaps Lord Ortolan didn't want to be the one to deliver
the order. That way, Count Alain had no opportunity to
frame him along with Phillip.

Neither he nor Maleficent had much time. Alain might
be arriving any minute.

Lord Ortolan's plan was remarkably good for being
so simple. Even if Aurora suspected the story wasn't true,

there would be no way to prove it once he and Maleficent were dead.

And every moment in the iron prison weakened her further, he was sure. He'd noticed that the instant after Lord Ortolan left, as the last soldier marched out with him, she sagged forward. It must have cost her a lot to hold herself together the way she had, to behave as though nothing touched her.

"How bad is it?" he asked softly.

"I'm well enough, Prince." Her voice sounded strained, as though she was speaking through gritted teeth. "Or I will be, just as soon as we are free."

"You're a bit terrifying," he said.

"Just a bit?" There was a smile in her voice.

"When I was a child, I saw a faerie—or at least I thought I did. It was a little thing, small enough to ride on the back of a bird. And I believed that if I caught it, it would give me a wish."

"Why should it do that?" Maleficent said irritably.

"My nurse told me stories about faeries that granted wishes," he returned. "And I didn't catch the faerie, of course. But no one even believed that I'd seen it. My mother told me to stop telling lies."

Maleficent was silent.

"My nurse said that if it had really been a faerie, it

would have bit me or put a spell on me." He gave a long, heavy sigh. "And that if I ever truly saw one, I ought to kill it. So I decided I'd dreamed it."

"If you are imagining I can wish us out of this, king's son, you are much mistaken," said Maleficent.

"When I saw Aurora for the first time, I thought per-haps she was one of you—one of the faeries of legend. She seemed like the answer to a wish. Like a dream. I believed I loved her instantly."

Maleficent snorted.

"You're right. I was infatuated. And that callow, love-lorn youth is who you see when you look at me, but I have lived at the palace for months. I have been by Aurora's side all that while. I have seen her goodness. I have sat with her in the garden when she cannot sleep at night for fear she won't wake."

Maleficent made a soft sound at that.

"I do love her. And you need not believe me, but I am going to prove it to you, when I get both of us out of here and save her."

"You are perhaps not as repulsive a suitor for Aurora as I thought you were," Maleficent said faintly. "But I will like you better still if you can keep that vow."

Phillip had made it impulsively and meant it abso-lutely, but that wasn't the same as having a plan. And it seemed all he could think of were the things Maleficent would be able to do if only she weren't surrounded by iron, like bending the bars or perhaps turning him into an ant the way she had turned Diaval into a dragon. Then he could walk out of the prison, get the keys, and free her.

The more he thought and thought without having a single useful idea, the more he felt like the callow youth he had denied being.

But then, after all, he did have an idea.

He would wager that just as Maleficent had entertained an idea of who he was, the guards did, too. They had heard Lord Ortolan call him a prince. So he would behave like one.

"Hey!" he shouted. "Guards! Hullo!"

"What are you doing?" Maleficent hissed.

"I'm cold and hungry," he informed her, pitching his voice loudly enough to be heard outside the room, "and unused to hardship."

After a few minutes of Phillip's shouting as loudly as he could, a guard entered, bearing a torch.

For a moment, the light was so bright that it was painful to Prince Phillip's eyes. He blinked against it, scowling. But now he could see the room. And he could see that another guard had come in after the first, this one with a set of iron keys dangling from his belt—the same iron keys he'd noticed when Lord Ortolan was giving his speech.

"What's all this howling for?" asked the guard with the torch.

"We require water and food and blankets," Phillip said in his best approximation of what people thought a petulant prince ought to sound like.

The guards laughed. "Oh, do you now, Your Highness? I suppose you think we're servants at your beck and call?"

"I imagine that your master would like the full ransom from Ulstead rather than the war he will get if I go missing in the kingdom of the Moors." The guards shared a glance. *No,* Phillip thought. Between that look and Lord Ortolan's words, he could tell they knew he was never intended to go home. "You can't expect me to believe that ridiculous story we were told about murder. No one would wish to begin their reign by inviting their neighbor to make war on them."

"You're probably right," agreed one of the guards.

"And," continued Phillip, "even a doomed man is given a last meal. Should your master really mean to put a period to my life, I can't believe he would do so without feeding me decently."

One of the guards shoved his torch into a holder with a sigh, relenting. "I'll see what I can find you, Prince."

He went out, which left only one guard—the one with the keys.

Perfect.

"What of her?" Prince Phillip said, gesturing toward Maleficent.

"The faerie?" asked the guard, peering at her through the bars as though looking at a dangerous beast.

"You can't possibly mean to leave me in here with her."

"Scared?" the guard asked.

"Look here," Phillip said, beckoning him over. "She's very ill and she's constantly moaning with pain. It's distressing."

"I will suck the marrow from your bones," Maleficent shouted, looking up at him with raw anger and showing her teeth. "Then you would know distress."

Phillip felt a rush of pure primal fear. The guard startled, too. In that moment, Phillip shoved his hand through the gap between bars and grabbed hold of the key ring. He pulled it as hard as he could. It came away in his hand, ripping loose from the leather of the guard's belt.

"Now see here," the guard said. "I was trying to help!"

"I am rebuked," Phillip admitted, putting a key into the latch and turning. Nothing happened. He tried a second key and the iron door swung open with a groan.

The guard had his sword drawn, but he seemed to barely notice Phillip racing past him to grab for a torch. The guard was too focused on Maleficent, who was rising from the ground and moving toward him, her full lips drawn into a wide and terrible smile, her inhuman eyes shining with monstrous glee.

He was still busy staring at her when Phillip clobbered him in the back of the head with the torch. The guard dropped to the floor, unconscious.

The other guard raced into the room. With a single wave of Maleficent's hand, he went flying against the back wall of the prison. She waved again, sending the unconscious guard across the floor and through the open door to the cell.

The door shut with a ringing clang.

"Wait," cried the guard Phillip had not knocked on the head. "You can't just leave us here."

"No?" Maleficent asked, her hand going to the stone wall as she swayed slightly. She was obviously not at her full strength, although she spoke with the confidence of someone who was. "I think you'll find that we're delighted by the prospect. A shame you didn't better provision us. Had you brought us a single luxury, it would now be yours."

And with that, she swept out of the room, leaving Phillip to follow her.

"That was well done," she told him in the hall.

"I am not sure it counts as a plan if my only thought was to keep talking until they made a mistake," he said, surprised by the praise.

"We're free," she said, "so it must."

Unfortunately, other than the set of keys and the torch, they had gotten hold of nothing that might be considered a weapon. Nor did Phillip have any idea where they were. Somewhere on Count Alain's lands, he guessed. That would account for a quantity of iron so great that a prison could be made of it.

He didn't like to think of how long the prison had been there or who had been kept in it before they had.

The hall had several doors identical to the one they'd come from and a central area where a few chairs surrounded a table with dice scattered across it. Phillip used the set of keys to unlock two more doors, finding the cells empty. But opening a third revealed a boy, who leaped to his feet as they entered.

"P-Prince Phillip?" the boy asked.

He sounded frightened. Phillip supposed he might well be afraid. What reason did he have to think that Prince

Phillip wasn't in league with Count Alain? "Yes, and I mean you no harm. I'm going to let you out."

"Oh, thank you, my lord," the boy said gratefully. Then he noticed Maleficent. She had remained in the hall, probably wanting to stay as far from the iron as possible, but her horned shadow loomed large in the room. He blanched.

Phillip opened the door to the cell. "Who are you and how did you come to be here?"

"My name is Simon, my lord," the boy said, emerging into the room. "I was a groom in the palace. I looked after your horse before, and I must say she's quite a goer."

Phillip smiled, a little amused. But he recognized the boy's name, and he could see that Maleficent did, too. He was the one whose family thought that he'd been taken by the faeries.

Simon went on, following Phillip into the hall. "I was in the stables and I overheard a conversation between Lord Ortolan and Count Alain. It was about the queen and it wasn't very nice. I thought I'd kept mum and they hadn't noticed me there, but a day later, when I was headed for home, soldiers surrounded me, and the next thing I knew, I was here."

"We'll get you out of this," Phillip promised.

Maleficent knelt down in front of the boy. He looked

panicky, and his fear only increased when she brought a fingernail beneath his chin. "Yes, child, we will help you, but not as you are. It's too dangerous."

"What do you—" the boy began.

"You can't—" Phillip started, realizing the only meaning her words could have.

"Into a rodent." Another wave of her hand and before them was a little mouse. He squeaked and made to run, but she lifted him by his tail.

"Here," she said to Phillip. "Put him in your pocket. He probably likes you better anyway."

Phillip stared at her in horror, but he took the mouse and cupped his hands around him. He could feel the trembling of the little body and the racing of the tiny heart. "Why did you do that?"

"I'm helping," she said with a pout. "He's in less danger as a mouse. And we're in less danger without having to worry he will do something foolish."

With a sigh, Phillip lifted his cupped hands to eye level. "Don't worry, Simon. She'll change you back as soon as we're out of the prison. I promise. And until then, you can sit on my shoulder."

Maleficent was already walking up a rough-cut stone staircase, taking a torch from the wall to light her way. Phillip followed, trying to ignore the feeling of tiny claws digging into his skin, even through the fabric of his shirt. "That's right," he murmured. "Hold on tight."

They stepped onto a landing of hewed stone, and Phillip realized where they must be. They were not just on Count Alain's land. This was one of his iron mines. No wonder Maleficent had been suffering.

There were carts piled with ore, waiting to be unloaded. And there was the wide opening of a man-made cave, leading out to a forest at night. Stars dotted the sky, and the scent of fresh air filled Phillip's lungs.

There was a guardhouse near that opening. From it, three soldiers emerged, along with Lord Ortolan.

Phillip cursed softly. Maleficent threw down her torch, obscuring them from view.

"Who's there?" the advisor called in a voice wavering with alarm.

The guards advanced toward the fallen light. They were armored, whereas the jailers below had not been. Phillip thought he recognized one of them as the soldier who'd stabbed him in the side. As they got closer, all drew iron blades.

"Stay hidden," Maleficent whispered to him. "Get out once the fighting begins. Steal a horse and find Aurora."

"What about you?"

"With any luck I will best them and beat you there,"

she whispered, her eyes lit with wild torchlight. "I travel faster than you ever shall."

Phillip wasn't bad with a blade, but he did the sort of fencing that distinguished a nobleman. He was used to a saber, not a heavy broadsword like the ones the guards were carrying.

And he had neither weapon.

Maleficent's mouth turned up into a smile and she walked forward, leaving Phillip hesitating. Should he follow her instructions? He slid toward the far wall of the mine and the shadows there.

No one was looking at him. They were staring at Maleficent as she walked into the torchlight and lifted her hands. A great wind whooshed from her fingertips, knocking the guards over and sending even Lord Ortolan to his knees. Even with all the iron around her, her magic was still something to behold.

With two powerful beats of her wings, Maleficent landed in front of Lord Ortolan, catching him by the throat.

She lifted her other hand, glowing with sparking green magic.

The other guards were getting slowly to their feet again, but they didn't dare approach—not when she had Lord Ortolan in such a vulnerable position. If they went for her, she could snap his neck.

And with another blast of her magic, it was settled. Their helmets clanked together, and this time when they went sprawling on the floor, they stayed there.

"Where is Prince Phillip?" Lord Ortolan demanded. "Phillip! If you can hear me, I know it wasn't sporting to lock you up, but that's all I ever intended. I said the rest to frighten you."

"A rather unlikely tale," Maleficent said. "But it hardly matters. As you can see, Phillip isn't here."

"I am an old man—a loyal advisor to Aurora's father and her grandfather before him. Aurora wouldn't like to see me harmed."

"Aurora isn't here, either," said Maleficent. "It's only you and I and your lackeys. But I don't think they will save you."

"You wouldn't dare!" Lord Ortolan sputtered, but the panic in his face was telling. And Phillip wasn't sure what to think. He wasn't certain what Maleficent might do right then.

She gave an extravagant shrug. "No point in debating when the answer is so close to hand. Let's find out."

"She means to murder me!" Lord Ortolan shouted. "Phillip, please. I am human, like you! Save me from this monster!"

"Prince Phillip is *gone*, dear Lord Ortolan," Maleficent

said, fixing the advisor with her startling emerald eyes. "I sent him away for just this reason."

Phillip realized that though they had been on the same side back in the prison, he wasn't sure they still were. He couldn't stand there and allow her to kill a person—or several persons—when it was within her power to take them prisoner.

But he wasn't at all sure he could stop her, either.

"Maleficent." A voice rang out near the entrance. There was a man with a skunk stripe of white in his hair and a blade on his hip. It seemed that Count Alain had finally returned.

29

Aurora woke to Diaval pecking at her fingers.

"*Ow!*" she cried, sitting upright and putting her hurt finger in her mouth. "Oh, you're back. Where were you?"

She turned toward where Count Alain had been sleeping, but he was no longer there. Only a tangle of blankets remained. Her dream was still thrumming through her mind, confusing her thoughts. She still saw the pallor of Prince Phillip's half-buried face, still heard his final shout echoing in her ears.

Run!

At the memory, she scrambled up out of her blankets. Diaval took off into the air.

Her dream confirmed for her that in her heart she didn't believe Phillip was to blame for Maleficent's disappearance. Aurora *knew* him. She believed that he was still the person she'd fallen in love with despite herself, someone kind and decent and good. She could believe he'd gone back to Ulstead, but she could never believe he would hurt anyone just for power or revenge.

Count Alain's words had played into her fears, but that didn't make them true.

And if I'm wrong, then nothing is fair, she told herself, *because we didn't even get a love story. He didn't kiss me one time when I was awake. If he was going to betray me, he should have at least kissed me first.*

With those thoughts in her head, Aurora followed the raven. As she walked, she noticed the imprints of boots on the ground. Count Alain must have gone the same way.

Her heart beat harder, the dream and her reality blending.

Through the woods she walked. Diaval moved silently above her, winging from tree to tree. They went past the spot where Diaval had stopped before. Along the way, she lost Alain's footprints, and the moonlight wasn't bright enough for her to find them again. She hoped that she wasn't lost.

"You know where we're going, right, Diaval?" she whispered.

But all he could do was caw in return.

As she walked on, she came to a place with steam rising from the ground. Frowning, she knelt, expecting to find a passage to hot springs beneath the earth, but there seemed to be a chimney there, venting up from the ground.

What was below them? Could her godmother be held there?

She nearly shouted for her, when her sense got the better of her fear. She was going to have to find a different way.

On she went until she found the path again. It forked, one part winding on through the woods and another cutting down into a quarry.

She recalled Count Alain's words: *We are not so far from my estate. Let's make for it in the morning. I will put my soldiers at your disposal.*

If they were close to his estate, then they were also close to his iron mines.

She found her way down the path in the moonlight, wishing with each step that she had an easy means of sending information to Smiling John. Wishing she'd come up with a different plan. Wishing she hadn't tried to be quite so clever.

Because there, gaping in front of her, was the entrance to the mine. She crept toward it. The closer she got, the more she was sure she heard voices. She peered into the smoky torchlit darkness, blinking and trying to make out shapes.

Several guards were lying on the ground some distance from Maleficent, who had her hand around the neck of a flailing Lord Ortolan.

"Godmother!" Aurora said, relief flooding her. She was so happy to see that her godmother was safe, alive, and unharmed that she failed to notice the warning in Maleficent's expression until it was too late.

"Run!" Maleficent said in a terrible echo of her dream. *Run. He's right behind you. Run!*

She spun around only to crash into Count Alain. He grabbed hold of her. She kicked as he hauled her up into the air, and she struck him with her fists until he caught them, twisting her arms behind her back.

"I am very sorry to do this, Your Majesty," he said. "Very sorry indeed. I had hoped to bring you to my home. I hoped we would grow close. I hoped you would never need to know about any of this. Even when you rode out,

I hoped I would be able to steal away and arrange everything before you awakened."

"Count Alain, what have you done?" Aurora asked.

"If only you'd listened to me. If only you had let me share my wisdom and experience, I wouldn't have had to resort to such drastic measures."

She looked at Maleficent and took a deep, shuddering breath. "Phillip was never a part of this, was he?"

"The prince was captured with me," Maleficent said. "But fear not, he's far from here. And he knows the truth of what you've done, Alain."

Relief washed over Aurora. Not only was Phillip not responsible for what had happened to Maleficent, but he was safe. He was free.

"I will be sure to send my men to track him," sneered Alain. "They always enjoy a hunt."

Aurora tried to pull away from Alain again. He held her fast, his gaze going to Maleficent. "As you can see, I have the queen in my power. If you don't want her harmed, release Lord Ortolan."

Maleficent let the old man fall. "You dare much, threatening your queen." He scuttled back from her, making a wheezing sound.

"The man who dares little achieves little," said Count

Alain. "Now, Lord Ortolan, I believe you will find iron chains in the guardhouse. Lock the faerie in them."

Maleficent raised hands sparking with magic as green as her eyes. She looked at Alain with a wild fury in her face. Then her gaze went to Aurora. Their eyes met and the light of her magic extinguished. She bent her horned head and smiled ruefully.

"You have found my weakness. Anything else and I would have brought down this cave on us both before I submitted."

30

Maleficent stood stoically as the guards approached.

"Don't do this for me, Godmother," Aurora pleaded, but Maleficent turned her gaze away. It was too easy for her to believe that Count Alain might alter his plans to include Aurora's death in them. She cursed herself for worrying more about Aurora's heart than about her head.

She looked out into the darkness and wished she hadn't sent Phillip away. She'd thought it was safer for him to go—and it had been. She just hadn't been concerned about the danger to her. She'd thought that she

HEART OF THE MOORS

could terrify Lord Ortolan into confessing to Aurora back at the palace.

And yes, she'd supposed that it was possible for Alain to show up while she was doing it. In fact, she'd rather hoped he would. She would have liked to present them both to Aurora, begging to tell her their evil schemes, all tied up in a bow.

She'd never expected Aurora to come herself.

Willful. Hadn't she said that was the girl's trouble? As for Diaval, when she found him, she was going to pluck every feather from his body. How could he be so foolish as to lead Aurora here, straight into danger?

Maleficent hissed as the iron touched her. Lord Ortolan only grinned at her like a beast baring his teeth as he clasped the iron manacles on her wrists. His pleasure as he turned the heavy key was evident.

She hoped that there would be bruises on his throat from her hands. But even that was small comfort.

Count Alain said, "Here's what we will do, dear Aurora. You will become my bride—"

"I will not!" Aurora spat. "You can't possibly believe I would ever consent."

The count smiled mirthlessly. "Oh, I rather think you will. You see, I am going to keep your godmother here to guarantee your good behavior. You will marry me and you will be my loyal queen — or this wicked faerie you love so much will pay for your every rebellion, no matter how small. This is not what I would have chosen, Aurora, but as I think of it, perhaps this is better. You might never love me, but you will never betray me, either."

Aurora struggled in Count Alain's arms. Maleficent had seldom felt so helpless — and, with her wings returned to her, had thought she'd never feel so helpless again.

She wanted to tell Aurora to refuse him, but then what? He had them both in his power. Better for Aurora to tell him what he wanted to hear and survive. Back at the palace, she could order that his head be chopped off.

"I will marry you," Aurora said finally, "but only if you let Maleficent go. My godmother will promise to stay in the Moors and not interfere with us, and I will promise to be docile and good."

"Impossible," Maleficent snapped reflexively.

Aurora frowned at her.

"Ah, Aurora, unfortunately, you believe me to be far kinder than I am. If it's any comfort, I fear your godmother is quite right. I doubt it would be possible for her to keep her promise not to interfere, and I don't mean to ask her to try."

Maleficent smiled at his assumption that that was the only bit she thought unlikely. But he went on, oblivious.

"I think you will be a most obliging queen with your godmother's life always in the balance," Count Alain said. "Almost as obliging as she was, letting herself be chained up for your sake."

"Quite a strategy, to leverage love against itself," said Lord Ortolan.

True love.

That was the cruel turn of phrase Maleficent had come up with as Stefan begged for her to remove the curse on Aurora. It was the thing she'd thought of as impossible.

But now, even as it bound her and Aurora, it still felt like a miracle that there was such a thing.

True love.

Love between people who took care of each other.

She'd been wrong to try to convince Aurora to protect her heart to the exclusion of all else. There was nothing wrong with Aurora's willfulness or her sweet nature. There was nothing wrong with Aurora's trying to see the best in people. There was nothing wrong with her generous heart. Those were all the things Maleficent had always loved about her. And if Maleficent had to spend her whole life locked in darkness and iron knowing that Aurora was free, it would have been worth it.

But she would not spend her life in darkness and iron knowing that Aurora was also in chains.

31

Lord Ortolan approached Count Alain and Aurora. "Come now, you've held the girl like that long enough. Her arms must be in agony. And there's no danger. The faerie is locked up, and there's nowhere for our little queen to go. Be chivalrous to your bride."

Alain eased his grip, and Aurora pulled away from him. Stumbling, she fell to her knees, humiliated and hurting.

"I am going to perform the ceremony marrying you and Count Alain before we leave the cave. I hope you understand that this is a formality," Lord Ortolan said. "It doesn't matter if you consent or not, but it would be better for all of us if we observe the proprieties."

Aurora wanted to spit in his face, but she knew that she had to wait for the right opportunity to get away from them.

Count Alain smiled at her. "You are very angry with me now, but I think we will grow used to each other. I am not so much of a monster when you get to know me."

She knew him well enough, she thought. She certainly knew he was a monster.

Count Alain guided her to stand to one side of Lord Ortolan, then stepped back a few paces.

Lord Ortolan cleared his throat.

Before he could get a sentence out, Phillip stepped out of the shadows. He was carrying a sword.

"Apologies," he said. "I didn't mean to take so long. First I had to sneak into the guardhouse and find a blade. Then I had to wait until Alain let you go. What a lot of dull speeches you've endured!"

Despite the horror of the situation, Aurora laughed.

"Oh, and the mouse," Phillip went on completely non-sensically. "I had to find a safe place for the mouse."

Count Alain's hand went to his own sword hilt.

"I thought I told you to leave," said Maleficent, although she didn't sound particularly displeased.

"As a prince," said Phillip, his gaze on Count Alain, "I practically have a duty to defy the commands of a foreign power."

Count Alain sneered, circling Phillip. "You ought to have run when you had the chance. You're, at most, a dilettante at the art of swordplay. But my family mines iron. Steel is my birthright. I am going to enjoy this."

"Embarrassing to you if I so much as get a hit in, then," said Phillip, moving into a fighting stance, holding his sword in front of him, the blade tipped slightly forward.

Alain matched him.

Lord Ortolan moved toward Aurora. "My dear, this is useless—"

She punched him in the mouth. She'd never hit anyone before, and it hurt her knuckles. But she had the satisfaction of seeing him stagger back, utterly shocked. He pressed a hand to the corner of his mouth, which looked a little red. One of his teeth must have cut the inside of it.

She felt a bit shocked, too, but it didn't stop her from prying the key out of his other hand.

Phillip and Alain traded blows back and forth, striking and parrying with a terrifying intensity, their blades whistling through the air. They looked evenly matched.

But as Phillip turned, she saw that blood soaked his

side. Looking closer, she saw a binding of ripped cloth around his waist. A wound he'd already had, then. A wound he'd reopened.

No matter how good he was with a blade, he wasn't going to be able to fight for long like that.

Aurora ran to Maleficent's side and slid the key into the lock of her manacles. As the iron slid off her pale wrists, two bands of blistered red skin showed.

"Don't worry about me, beastie," Maleficent said with a smile, but Aurora couldn't help noticing how slowly she moved.

The iron chain, with manacles on each side, was heavy in Aurora's hand. She looked at Count Alain.

Phillip lost his footing. It was just a small stumble, perhaps from his boot hitting a rock, but it was enough for Alain to strike, shoving his sword into Phillip's wound. Phillip pivoted out of the way before the blade could sink into his side, but even the graze of the tip made him gasp in pain. He brought up his sword just in time to parry a blow that would have run through his heart.

Holding on to one manacle, Aurora swung the other at Alain's back. It hit him hard, sending him sprawling onto the floor of the mine. Phillip turned his blade, the point at Alain's throat.

Lord Ortolan walked forward but stopped at a fierce

look from Maleficent. Aurora went to him and held out the manacles, her heart racing. "Give me your hands," she said.

The old man looked mutinous.

"Step to it." There was a new voice. Diaval walked into the cave and nodded to Aurora, rolling his shoulders. "Yes, it's me, finally with thumbs and a tongue fit for speaking. As soon as Maleficent had her hands free, I started hopping around the entrance, hoping she'd see me. Better late than never, Diaval is here to help."

"I should have broken your neck when I had the chance," Count Alain said to Phillip, ignoring the new arrival.

"You're a fool," Phillip returned, looking down at him. "You had wealth. You had influence. You had the ear of a queen. And because you could not see what you had, you will have nothing."

Aurora noticed that Phillip looked very pale, almost like he had in her dream. There was even a touch of blue to his lips.

"I played the same game you're playing," Alain spat at him. "Just because you played it better, that's no reason to sneer at it." With those words, he pushed aside Phillip's blade and lifted his own to strike.

Aurora screamed. There was no way Phillip would react in time.

"Into a bug." Maleficent waved her hand, and in a wild rush of glittering gold magic, Alain was no longer there. In his place was a large black centipede. His sword fell with a clang beside it.

Phillip lifted Alain's blade from the ground, squinting at the centipede. "He's going to be difficult to catch if he crawls up on the ceiling," he said, then sagged to the floor. The blood from his wound had soaked all the way to his boot.

"Phillip!" Aurora shouted.

"Oh, no, don't worry about me," he said faintly. "I'll have a little lie-down and then be fine—"

"Don't be more of a fool than usual," Maleficent told him. "We need to rebind your side. Diaval, go find me some yarrow, the crumblier the better."

"Yes, mistress. No need, by the by, to thank me for bringing Aurora to your rescue," he said. "No need for me to have freed myself and thought of nothing but coming back here, flying through the night and day. No, no need to thank me at all."

Maleficent gave him a fierce look. "You mean for bringing Aurora straight into danger?"

Aurora left them bickering and knelt beside Phillip. "If you move onto your side," she said, "it will elevate the wound and help slow the bleeding."

As he turned, she pillowed his head onto her lap. He looked up at her and gave her a lazy smile. She stroked his hair back from his brow, her heart aching.

"I do love you," she told him. "I was afraid to tell you that. I was afraid to admit it to myself. But I do."

Afraid the way she was frightened to fall asleep at night, because it felt like giving in to something she couldn't control.

Or the way humans were frightened of faeries. Love was as unpredictable and powerful as any magic. But maybe it was also as marvelous.

His smile grew. "Now I know I must be delirious, since the only time you say things like that is in my dreams."

In the distance, there was the sound of horns.

32

S miling John arrived soon after, one of his scouts having discovered Aurora and Alain's camp and tracked them from there. He found an exhausted group resting beneath a newly grown tree, its limbs shimmering with magic and some of its roots formed into a mossy, bark-covered cage that held an enormous scuttling black centipede. On the other side, the roots seemed to have grown over Lord Ortolan's ankles, holding him in place.

"My queen," Smiling John said, bowing stiffly, "your leaving your camp after dark had us in quite a panic. We came as soon as we got a signal from the raven, but —"

He looked around and swallowed the rest of the lecture he had clearly been planning on giving. "I see you have everything well in hand."

Maleficent eyed them with suspicion. "How do you come to be looking for her?"

"Queen Aurora ordered us to follow behind her with a large battalion and to await a summons from the bird. She said she thought she was going into a trap, but she couldn't be certain who had set it. She suspected the count but believed that the only way to prove it was to go along with the scheme and see who the traitors were and what they were planning. I disagreed, as I thought it was too great a risk. But in the end, it seems she was correct."

Maleficent eyed Aurora with an obvious desire to scold her. "So you knew you were going into danger —"

"I knew *you* were in danger," Aurora reminded her.

Smiling John went on. "A rider came to tell us that Lady Fiora turned in packets of letters between her brother and Lord Ortolan. We were very worried for you, Your Majesty."

Aurora recalled Lady Fiora trying to prevent her from traveling with Count Alain. At the time, she had just thought Lady Fiora didn't want her to leave the party, not that she was trying to save her from her brother's schemes.

"I would not have thought it of her," she remarked softly to herself.

Smiling John's people bustled about, trying to make Phillip more comfortable and telling him how fortunate he was that the wound hadn't been deeper or in a different spot.

Phillip, for his part, was trying to prevent Diaval from being the one to hold Simon.

"Give me the mouse," Phillip called, "right now. Aurora, make a royal proclamation that the mouse is for me to hold until your godmother turns him back."

"You don't trust me not to eat him?" Diaval asked with a raised brow, letting the rodent run up one arm and onto the other, his gaze following the movement with a disturbing fixedness.

"I do not," Prince Phillip said.

"You are the one who ate a mouse heart, I should remind you," said Diaval, bringing his head eye level with a terrified Simon, who stopped running. "He did, you know. Gobbled it right up."

"It was *one time*," Phillip protested.

Maleficent allowed the royal guard to take Lord Ortolan from her tree prison into the cart. With a wave of her hand and a whorl of glittering golden magic, both he and the cage of roots that held Count Alain the centipede were loosed from the tree. The guards walked around the cage in confusion as to how to move it without getting close to the thing inside.

"Well, my queen, since we don't have your carriage, may we offer up our humble carts?" asked Smiling John. "I wish we had something more fitting, but we were moving too quickly to bring more."

"Oh, no," said Maleficent. "I will return them to the castle."

She gestured toward Diaval, and gold sparked at her fingertips.

He threw up his hands as though he could block the magic. "Wait, what exactly are you planning on turning me into this time? You ought to ask my permission for these things. It had better not be a dog!"

"I doubt you'll mislike this so very much." She waved her hand, and he grew longer and larger until a black horse stood in his place. From the sides of his back, enormous shimmering raven wings unfurled. And from his mane, a mouse peeped out.

The guards sucked in their breath, perhaps thinking of the dragon she'd once turned him into, perhaps just awed by such magic. Maleficent smiled her widest and most sinister smile.

"You should do something about Simon first," Phillip said. "I don't think he ought to be flying. Perhaps he can return with the guard."

"Very well. *Into a boy.*" Maleficent gestured with a negligent wave of her hand, and in a wash of shimmering gold, Simon was human again.

He fell off the horse's back, stumbling as he moved into a standing position. The poor boy was clearly getting used to not being on all fours. He looked around, then saw Aurora and bowed hastily.

"The missing lad!" Smiling John said. "So he *was* under a faerie curse."

With so much attention on him, Simon sputtered a little. "No, sir," he said. "Or at least, I was, but only for this past little while. The elf lady and Prince Phillip freed me from a cell where I've been locked for days and days. She thought I'd be safer traveling in a pocket and turned me into a mouse, which I'm sorry to say I didn't like above half." He paused with a look at Maleficent. "Not that I don't appreciate it, though, for you've done me nothing but a good turn."

Smiling John's gaze went to the cage and the centipede inside, then to Maleficent. "I don't suppose that you'll turn *him* back."

"Of course she will," Aurora said over whatever

Maleficent was about to say. "Centipedes can't stand trial."

"Can't they?" Maleficent asked with a mischievous quirk of her mouth. "Are you sure?"

Aurora gave her a stern look.

"As soon as we're back in the palace, then?" Maleficent said.

Aurora's expression did not falter.

"Very well!" With an exasperated wave of her hand, the centipede grew larger and larger until its arms and legs broke through the cage and it returned to the shape of Count Alain. He looked ridiculous.

"John," Alain shouted, trying to shuck off the remains of the cage. It was remarkably hard to remove from his head. "You can't believe all this nonsense! She put a curse on me. You have to see that she's the one you should be putting in chains!"

Smiling John shook his head and spoke to Maleficent. "You may have had the right of it. If you'd left him as he was, we wouldn't have to hear his mouth all the way back to the palace."

With that, he headed off to his troops, steering Simon toward one of the mounted soldiers.

Diaval, in his winged-horse form, knelt down so that Phillip could more easily get onto his back. Phillip did, gingerly, and Aurora got up behind him.

Then, with a great sweep of his wings, Diaval pushed off the ground and they were flying. Higher and higher they climbed. Moments later, Maleficent was beside them, a wide smile on her face and a rare light in her eyes.

Maleficent was always graceful, but being in the air was her natural state, and she moved through it like a dancer. She dove and spiraled and flew with irrepressible joy. And her unfurled wings beat strong and steady on her back.

Phillip knotted his fists in the horse's mane. Aurora put an arm around the side of his waist that wasn't hurt, leaned back her head, and looked up at the clouds, her hair streaming behind her like a banner.

Aurora slept that night, out of sheer exhaustion. When she woke, dawn was just breaking on the horizon. She watched the sun come up and thought over what she needed to do. By the time Marjory entered with a breakfast tray, she had come to some decisions.

Marjory put the tray down, rushed to her, and clasped Aurora's hands. "Oh, I am so glad you're well. I was so worried."

"I was worried myself at times," Aurora admitted, squeezing Marjory's fingers.

Aurora drank her tea and ate a piece of bread with butter and listened as Marjory told her about dancing at the festival. She'd even gone around the maypole with one of the Fair Folk and blushed at telling Aurora some of the compliments he paid her.

After breakfast, Aurora put on a robe and went up the stairs to Prince Phillip's room. If they could meet in the middle of the night, then she wasn't going to stand on ceremony now, when she wanted to know how badly he'd been hurt.

She didn't expect to find him bare to the waist, having his wound rewrapped by an elderly doctor with wild white hair and long tufted sideburns.

"Oh, hello," Phillip said, clearly a little embarrassed.

Aurora felt her cheeks heat and tried hard to keep her eyes only on his shoulders. "I just wanted to make sure you're well."

"No dancing for a few weeks," he said. "But I've had stitches, and an ogre came over this morning bearing packets of a special tea in which I'm supposed to soak my bandages to speed healing."

Aurora glanced at the doctor, wondering if he was suspicious of faerie remedies.

He saw her look and smiled. "Once your treaty is signed, most of the people in Perceforest will be excited to trade for gems, but for me there is no greater treasure than the herbs of the Moors. Ones humans have not been able to gather for generations, but which are rumored to be able to cure many diseases that plague us."

"I hope you will come to the ceremony today," she told the doctor, and then gave Phillip a smile. "And I hope your patient will as well."

It was with a light step that Aurora returned to her room to get ready for the treaty-signing ceremony.

The pixies interrupted her on the stairs. They had a lot to tell her about, most of it regarding Nanny Stoat and how clever she was. Apparently, she had pressed Thistlewit, Flittle, and Knotgrass into service, getting them to do little magics around the castle and managing them with such flattery that they enjoyed it.

"You see," said Flittle, "Lord Ortolan never saw our importance in this kingdom."

"We should have known he was wicked then," added Thistlewit. "After all we've sacrificed, how could anyone not reward our loyalty?"

"Very right," Aurora agreed, smiling.

They also passed on some gossip. After depositing Aurora and Phillip at the castle, Maleficent had been convinced to go with Smiling John to return Simon to his family. Once the boy was done telling them about the awful Count Alain, they were not only trying to press tea and jam on Maleficent but paying her such flattering compliments that she had to flee in horror at their overwhelming gratitude.

"Although I don't know why they singled her out in such a way, when no one ever bothers to invite us for tea, even though we are much more agreeable," Knotgrass put in.

"A mystery, to be sure," Aurora said.

Aurora entered the throne room in cloth of gold, wearing her crown, and with a smile lingering at the corners of her mouth.

Already there were the Fair Folk. Maleficent and Diaval stood at the front, beside tree sentries, wallerbogs, hobs, ogres, hedgehog faeries, and more. Maleficent was in a long black gown, with silver bands on the horns of her head and matching ones on the horns at the joints of her wings. Diaval was in a long black coat with cuffs made of feathers that were undoubtedly his own. The pixies hastened to make a place for themselves at the front, buzzing their bright wings and forcing everyone else to move.

The humans were also assembled in the hall. There

were nobles, young and old, including Lady Sybil and Lady Sabine and a nervous-looking Lady Fiora. And Nanny Stoat was there, along with farmers and villagers. Simon stood beside his family, looking proud. She supposed that his story had been in great demand with everyone he met and that he had been made much of.

Aurora cleared her throat and began to speak. "Before me is a document that will set the terms of an enduring peace in our unified kingdom, one that I hope will live on past the end of my reign. It will be signed not just by me, but by representatives from the humans and the faeries. Will the representatives please come forward?"

Maleficent and Nanny Stoat moved to the sides of Aurora's carved wood throne. A small table was brought forward by a footman, and a scribe set down a long scroll on which the terms of the treaty were set out.

"Some of you may know that a conspiracy to prevent this was undertaken by my advisor, and that was the reason for the delay in this ceremony," said Aurora. "If anyone here imagines attempting something similar, know that both conspirators are in prison and will remain there for long years.

"Furthermore, Lord Ortolan's wealth will be stripped from him and used to fund the distribution of rations of barley to anyone in Perceforest or the Moors in need of food. Once, he said such a thing was too costly for the royal treasury to undertake. I hope he will be pleased to know that because of him, it is now possible.

"As for Count Alain's estates, they will go to his sister, Lady Fiora. We hope to be better friends with her than we were with her brother, and we hold none of his actions against her."

Lady Fiora looked up at Aurora in surprise and gratitude. She sank into a deep curtsy.

"And now I am in the position of needing a new advisor," Aurora said.

Of all the decisions she'd had to make, this one was the most difficult. It was evident already that Nanny Stoat made a much better advisor than Lord Ortolan ever had—even setting aside the whole treason thing—and Aurora was tempted merely to install her in the position. But the more she thought about it, the more that didn't seem right, either. No one person could give her all the help she needed or represent everyone that needed representing.

"From now on, I will have not one advisor, but a chamber that will help me make decisions for these lands."

There were a few she was sure she was going to ask. Maleficent, obviously, but also Robin. And Nanny Stoat. Maybe the doctor. Perhaps Smiling John. She knew that when she was done, though, she would have collected people—faeries and humans—who were committed to changing Perceforest for the better.

"But first," said Aurora, "let us sign this treaty and agree to be good neighbors to one another."

Maleficent reached to yank a single shining black feather from the cuff of Diaval's coat. He made a sharp noise of pain, and Aurora decided that they must be his feathers after all, especially once she saw that Maleficent had signed in shining red blood that was already drying brown.

"We will do as you bid," Maleficent said, "and respect your laws. We won't sour anyone's milk or steal anyone's children"—her eyes twinkled—"so long as no one expressly agrees to a bargain involving those things."

Nanny Stoat stepped up to sign as well. "We humans will follow the laws set forth in this document. We will not steal from the Moors, nor will we harm any faeries we encounter in Perceforest." She fixed Maleficent with a look. "And we do not need to mention any exceptions."

Maleficent shrugged extravagantly, and Nanny Stoat signed with the white quill the scribe provided her, dipped in black ink.

Then it was Aurora's turn. She signed with black ink,

a quill of her own, and a great flourish. "And I myself promise to do whatever I can to promote peace between my people. To that end, I will split my time between my kingdoms. Half will be spent in the palace here, and half in my palace in the Moors. But wherever I am, I promise that humans and faeries will be welcome."

The room broke into applause. There were congratulations all around. Everyone wanted to speak with Aurora.

Lady Fiora wanted to beg Aurora's pardon for not telling her outright about her suspicions about her brother. Lady Sabine and Lady Sybil wanted to hear about Aurora riding to Phillip and Maleficent's rescue, which they seemed to think was both outrageous and a bit of a romantic adventure. And her pixie aunties wanted to tell her that while they liked the way she'd arranged her hair, they were sure they could magic it into a much better confection if only she'd let them.

Eventually, people began to file out.

As they did, Phillip walked toward Aurora. He was wearing a woolen doublet with a row of gold buttons up the middle and slashes showing a bright print underneath. His brown curls flopped over one eye, and his gentle smile didn't reveal anything. Had she not known he was hurt, she would never have guessed.

"You did it," he told her, "just like you said you would."

She grinned up at him. "I am glad you were here to see it happen."

"I have the oddest notion," he said, "that when I was losing a lot of blood, you told me something I very much wanted to hear. But maybe I misheard you. Or perhaps you were carried away by your concern for me. Perhaps you were afraid I was going to die —"

"I have another riddle for you," she said, interrupting him. "What is mine, but only you have it?"

She felt her cheeks grow hot. It was no matter that she'd already told him she loved him, even if he wasn't sure whether it was memory or wishful thinking. She was still shy to say it again.

"That's easy," he said. "My heart."

"No!" she told him. "It's supposed to be *my* heart."

"Are you certain?" he asked, his manner serious, giving the question greater weight.

"Yes," she said. "Even when you're not bleeding on the floor of a mine after being stabbed by my mortal enemy, I still love you."

"Oh," he said, looking as though he had suddenly become the shy one. "Thank goodness." He gave her hand a squeeze and moved toward the hall, where the other courtiers were heading. She would follow in a moment. But first there was something she had to do.

Aurora turned toward her godmother. Maleficent was watching Phillip depart. She raised her eyebrows at Aurora.

Aurora walked toward her. "You aren't still going to insist he's a mistake."

"If you suppose that because Prince Phillip turned out to be something of a hero, I am going to say that I like him, you are very much mistaken," Maleficent said, but there was a light in her eyes and a curve of her lip that belied the words.

"All that proves is that you are still my dear wicked godmother," Aurora said.

"And you are my fearless beastie," Maleficent told her. Then she amended the pronouncement. "My fearless *queen* beastie."

EPILOGUE

Would you like to know what it's like to have your wings again?

Imagine falling, except instead of hitting the ground, you soar.

Imagine beginning to believe that love is never a lie, even if there are liars.

Imagine recalling that cracked bone grows back stronger.

That scars are beautiful.

You might not be quite who you were when you lost the power of flight.

But it is only in having your wings resting heavy on your back again that you realize you always and forever belonged to the sky.

You were always strong and fierce and full of magic.

Even when you were stranded on the ground.

ACKNOWLEDGMENTS

S ome of the riddles were taken, in part, from *Anglo-Saxon Riddles of the Exeter Book*. A few were invented by me.

Thank you to Emily Meehan, Brittany Rubiano, and everyone at Disney for letting me play in this world and for making the process of writing this book so much fun. Thank you to Kelly Link, Cassandra Clare, Steve Berman, and Josh Lewis for quickly convening a workshop to help me fix the first draft. Thank you to Sarah Rees Brennan for all your great notes. And apologies to Ursula Grant, who would have given me great notes had I given her the chance. Thank you to my agent, Jo Volpe, for her encouragement and for figuring out an extremely tricky schedule. And huge thanks to my best beloveds, Theo and Sebastian, for making me endless cups of coffee and letting me hole up in my office to get this done.